Peaches
and
Smeets

Peaches
and
Smeets

ASHTI JUGGATH

modjaji books

A NOTE ON THE TERMINOLOGY

Pejorative terms such as 'coolie', and 'girl' and 'boy' for domestic workers and gardeners of any age, were used freely in official documentation and newspapers, and in casual conversation, in South Africa at the time some of this novel is set – the 1950s and 1960s. Historically accurate, these terms are also offensive. They have been used to support the narrative and remain true to the context of the story.

Ableist language, now unacceptable but commonly in use at the time this novel is set, is also employed within the chronological context of the story.

Place names are used as they were at the time in the narrative.

ༀ ༀ

Published in 2022 by Modjaji Books
Cape Town, South Africa
www.modjajibooks.co.za
© Ashti Juggath

Edited by Tracey Hawthorne
Cover artwork by Carla Kreuser
Text design and typesetting by User Friendly
Set in Stempel Garamond LT Pro 10.75 on 14.75 pt
Printed and bound by Creda Communications

ISBN 978-1-928215-96-7 (print)
ISBN 978-1-928215-97-4 (e-book)

To my children, Adiya, Vidur and Pranav

'Above all, be the heroine of your life, not the victim.'
— Nora Ephron

ജ 1 ର

1954: Arrivals and departures

Sitting in the front seat of the car, only her with her father, made Smita feel very important. For this outing, she'd been allowed to wear one of her favourite dresses, a royal-blue velvet one with a white satin lace-trimmed collar, and her shiny patent-leather shoes that made clickety-clack sounds when she walked. There were very few occasions when she was allowed to dress up – on her birthday, for family weddings and on Diwali – so this was definitely a treat.

She treasured these rare moments alone with Pitaji. For four years she'd been the only child, but then Shruthi had come along, and now there would be another baby soon.

The view was quite different from here, compared to when she was sitting in the back with her sister, even though she had to crane her neck a little to see out the windows and over the dashboard, despite having the privilege of sitting on Ma's pretty cushion. Eyes wide, she stared at the tall buildings in the town, the displays of the mannequins with their elegant clothes and shoes, and the colourful signs outside the shops. These shopfronts with their huge glass windows and the bold, fancy lettering depicting their names – John Orr's, Greatermans, Stuttaford's – were a welcome contrast to the otherwise mundane, drab landscape of the highveld.

Smita's family rarely ventured into Springs town, as most of their food shopping was done at the Indian-owned shops near their home in Bakerton, about five miles to the north. Smita's parents often seemed reluctant to go into what they referred to as 'the town shops', which was one of the many mysteries of adults that she could not unravel.

'Okay, Smeets, let's see how clever you are. Which room has no doors?' her father asked. His intention was to distract her from what lay ahead with riddles that she always found hilarious, but truth be told, with all the excitement of the drive, and having her father all to herself, she'd almost forgotten about her toothache and the trepidation of visiting the dentist.

Smita scrunched up her face in serious concentration – she didn't want to disappoint him. 'Um, I don't know, Pitaji,' she finally replied, a little anxiously.

'A mushroom!'

Smita giggled. 'Ask me another one.'

'Okay, next one. Why was six afraid of seven?'

Smita squinted her eyes and thought for a while before saying, 'I give up.'

'Because seven ate nine!' her father roared.

'Oh, Pitaji, you are so funny!' she said, her smile wide, looking at him with admiration.

When they reached the building where the dentist's offices were, Smita naturally thought they would climb the fancy marble stairs leading to the main arched entrance, but Pitaji directed her to the back of the building, to a rickety steel staircase and an ugly door. 'Why can't we go up there?' she asked her father, looking back over her shoulder at the fancy stairs.

'I'm sorry, Smeets, but the sign says that those stairs are only for white people.'

'But that's not what the sign said,' insisted Smita, who had seen the sign at the base of the fancy stairs. At the tender age of seven, she was just beginning to read fluently and knew the word 'net' and just assumed that they had spelt 'blankets' incorrectly, and thought that maybe they were selling net blankets nearby.

Her father sighed and looked at her kindly. 'The sign is in Afrikaans. "Net" means "only" and "blankes" means "whites". You need to get used to these things; we Indians are not treated the same as the white people in this country.'

Smita frowned. The explanation seemed unfair and ridiculous. But more of this became apparent when they reached the dentist's rooms. There were two sides of the waiting room, one furnished with plush chairs and the other with a wooden bench. Although Smita, in her pretty dress, wanted to sit in one of the plush chairs, her father shook his head and directed her to the wooden bench. She could not understand this, as all the fancy chairs were vacant, and were clearly more suitable for the way she was dressed, but, sensing the slightly stressed gravity in her father's gesture, she did as he directed.

There was only one other person in the waiting room, sitting at the other end of the bench: an impeccably dressed old man with wrinkly brown skin. He scared her a little, as he reminded her of the men she saw hanging around the shops smoking pipes that Martha, the family's live-in maid, referred to as 'daggarokers'. Noticing her discomfort, her father pulled her onto his lap and held her tightly.

Fortunately, they did not need to wait too long. The lady at the desk pointed her pen at her father and barked, 'Maharaj?' Her father nodded, and she said, 'You're next,' and pointed down a long corridor. 'The door at the end.'

The dentist was an old man with kind, blue eyes, bushy eyebrows and a welcoming smile. 'This is a little mirror,' he said, showing her a steel instrument with a disc at the end. 'I'm going to use it to look at your teeth. Open wide.' As he looked into her mouth, gently poking and prodding at the stubborn milk tooth that seemed to be preventing the permanent tooth from emerging, and causing her pain, she felt herself relaxing a bit.

Her father, sitting on a chair nearby, chatted to the dentist in Afrikaans – he was fluent in the language, as it was a subject he'd taught for many years. Lying in the chair, her eyes moving between the two men, Smita noticed for the first time how pale her father's skin was – almost as pale as the dentist's. It was markedly different from her own, which was light brown, like milky tea. Her mother's skin tone was a bit darker than hers – like milky coffee.

Afrikaans was a language largely unknown to Smita. It didn't sound too friendly, this language, and although she knew that she had to learn it at school, she wasn't looking forward to it. She had picked up some words of Afrikaans from Martha, as many African domestic workers and miners, especially in the Transvaal, learnt Afrikaans to communicate with their bosses. Their previous maid had spoken Fanagalo, a mélange of the most common languages spoken in South Africa, like Zulu, English, Afrikaans and a few other African languages, so that everyone could understand each other.

'It's not a serious problem and I don't want to cause her un-necessary pain, so I'm not going to extract the milk tooth,' the dentist said to her father in heavily accented English. 'It will not be long before it falls out, and until then, you can give her some of the pain syrup that they sell at the pharmacy if she finds it very uncomfortable.' Turning to Smita and beaming at her, he said, 'You have been so brave, little girl. I am done looking at your beautiful teeth. You must just be patient and wait for the tooth to fall out.'

When they left the room, Shankar also gave Smita a hug in a rare show of affection. 'I am so proud of you, Smeets: you were very brave, like the dentist said. But you are always very brave, my little brown-eyed girl.' He smiled at her and continued, 'I remember when you were a baby, your eyes were like mine – they could not decide if they were green or grey. But after a few months they turned this lovely light-brown colour. With those lovely eyes came your beautiful smile, which of course gave you your name.'

12

Smita had heard this story from both her parents many times before – smita was Sanskrit for 'smile'. But she never tired of hearing these stories from her father, and felt very special that he had a nickname for her. It was something between just the two of them.

The drive back home from the dentist wasn't as exciting as the journey there. Leaving behind the relative sophistication of the town, with its white-occupied suburbs around the city centre, Shankar's two-toned 1956 Chevy passed through endless fields of dried, brown grass interspersed with the equally depressing yellow mounds of the mine dumps. Bakerton, the 'Indian area' where the Maharaj family lived, was surrounded by these nondescript stretches of veld, and bordered by a railway line. The constant clatter and clanking of the railcars carrying coal from the mines to the goldfields closer to Johannesburg ran parallel to the Indian area, engulfing the area in a hazy cloud of smoke.

Between them and the town was Payneville, the designated area for black and some coloured people, mostly mine workers. Here, the malodorous stench of the paper mill permeated the air, the smog hanging overhead seeming to demarcate the area and physically separate it from the white homes closer to the town. But that was not the only barrier: at night the ominous sound of metal scraping tarmac announced that the gates barring any exit from this designated area were being closed; the same sound was heard again early in the morning, a signal that the residents could leave to go to their jobs.

In the car, Smita thought miserably about returning to Ma and her little sister, both of whom were often crabby these days. Since Ma announced that she was having another baby, it seemed as if she was always sick or tired. Then three-year-old Shruthi, sensing Ma's moods, would act up and demand attention. Ma would make Smita do more chores, instead of allowing her to meet her chums on the road and resume their game of three tins. Life didn't seem very fair lately.

Shankar was thoughtful as he drove, his normally cheerful countenance transformed into an uncharacteristic long face. Glancing sideways at his eldest daughter, sitting quietly in the passenger seat with her hands folded in her lap, he realised that his little girl was growing up, but having to try to explain some of the conditions and circumstances of this land where they lived to an innocent child had been disheartening. God worked in wondrous ways, he mused, so obviously there was a reason why the white man had been given superiority. And he could rationalise it all by saying that karma would take care of the injustices in the world, and that humans were here to fulfil a duty, and that therefore they had to endure all the trials and tribulations that life threw at them, but children would not understand that.

He'd been avoiding spending too much time at home lately. His wife, Subha, was increasingly irritable as the pregnancy progressed. This one was worse than the previous two; maybe it was her yearning for a male child that was causing her to be more highly strung. For her sake, he hoped that this wish of Subha's would be fulfilled. He'd tried to explain to her that it wouldn't reflect inadequacy on her part if she didn't produce a male heir, but she had some very fixed traditional ideas.

Anyway, these issues were not a priority for him right now. He was focusing on growing his portfolio as the local Hindu priest. Lots of people called on him to do their pujas, the religious rituals to ensure that the gods would smile down on them, so he felt like he was following his vocation, and honouring his promise to his father to continue to uphold the Brahmin legacy he'd inherited. And, all things considered, it was a blessing that he had this moonlighting opportunity, even if it was due partly to the good fortune of his caste status.

His father had made a decent income from his priestly duties, and had managed to buy some properties and invest in a fleet of taxis. With the inheritance left to him, Shankar had managed to set himself up quite well but he felt he still needed to make more money for his growing family to live in comfort. The salary of a schoolteacher was simply not adequate for certain luxuries.

The only problem was that, even though he was generating this additional income, Subha was unhappy that he had to socialise after he'd performed the prayer ceremonies, either in private homes or in the local temple, and this meant that he often didn't get home until late. But Shankar felt that in order to maintain and, he hoped, increase his congregation, nurturing these relationships was as vital as the actual service he provided.

He sighed to himself. At least the socialising prevented him from focusing on the problems at home, he thought – the constant complaining from Subha about the big house, which was often cold and which she found difficult to keep clean, the two children who demanded all her attention, and their eldest daughter who apparently did not help enough. He didn't agree with this last point, as he firmly believed that children should be allowed to be children for as long as possible, but to disagree would cause Subha to rant and rave about how he wasn't home often enough to help, and to then become extremely emotional about having left her home and her support structures far away in Natal.

It was constantly surprising to Shankar that, on the one hand, Subha was a dutiful, traditional Indian wife, but, on the other, she could be so feisty at times. It was, of course, one of the many reasons he felt so much affection for her, for to have a partner who was meek and mild would have been unfulfilling for him. He counted himself fortunate that Subha, who was ten years his junior, was not the traditional subservient Indian wife who allowed herself to be treated as a doormat. For all her complaints, she was an intelligent woman who deserved his respect and could make many of her own decisions.

Just sometimes, though, she tended to be too forceful and steadfast in her beliefs about how they presented themselves to society, and about the image of the perfect Brahmin family that they projected to the community. Shankar knew this image was important for the role he played but there was a limit to the dramatisation he was prepared to enact to achieve the appropriate representation of it.

'I know – let's stop and get a packet of chips and some Coo-ee,' he said suddenly to Smita.

'Ma won't like that,' Smita said, but she was already grinning in anticipation of the forbidden treat.

'She doesn't have to know,' Shankar said, and wiggled his eyebrows conspiratorially before they both burst out laughing.

Back home, as soon as she opened the front door, the delicious aroma of freshly baked bread wafted through. It made Smita's tummy growl with expectation, despite the crisps and cooldrink she'd just gobbled up in the car.

She ran to the kitchen to find Ma leaning against the doorway for support for her expanding tummy but looking radiant.

'My big baby is back!' her mother said, opening her arms for Smita to run into them. 'Shruthi has been asleep for most of the afternoon, and I felt a sudden burst of energy, so I made your favourite, my sweetheart – fresh bread and stew. Since you went to the dentist, I thought that maybe you'd need something soft to eat, and I know how much you love bread straight from the oven.'

'Oh, Ma!' Hugging her mother, Smita felt a lump form in her throat from all the bad things she'd assumed would happen when she arrived home. 'You're the best!'

At that moment, Shruthi tottered into the kitchen with Pitaji. She'd waited patiently at the front door for him after he'd parked the car, and Smita was grateful for the distraction, as her eyes were brimming with tears of guilt.

A little later, gathered around the big kitchen table adorned with the embroidered floral tablecloth, the family feasted together. The kitchen was a spacious room, with the cast-iron coal stove in one corner that burned all winter, heating the space as well as cooking their food, and was also used in summer for food prep.

Smita looked up at her mother's beaming face and felt a rush of emotion. She deeply admired her mother, with her flawless milky-coffee complexion, large expressive cocoa-brown eyes that were now filled with warmth but could turn fierce and piercing when she was angry, and soft ebony hair pulled back with the middle parting always anointed with vermilion sindoor to indicate her married status. Even with her pregnancy face, which was plumper than usual, and with her somewhat swollen nose, she was still beautiful.

Smita's gaze moved to her father, whose greenish-grey eyes were full of adoration for her mother. In her mind, her father was the handsomest man who had ever existed. He looked like one of the kings in her books, with his long, angular face, high forehead, strong mouth and slightly wavy hair with its distinct light-brown undertones. Smita wondered again why his skin was so much paler than that of the rest of the family.

She saw a lot of her father in herself: she was also tall for her age, and lanky, with the fairer colouring and lighter hair that her mother was always commenting on. Shruthi resembled their mother, with her apple-cheeked, heart-shaped face, which still had the plumpness of baby fat, her silky shiny hair, and those angelic eyes that endeared her to everyone.

The little family of four, safe in the warm kitchen while the highveld winter night gripped the landscape outside, chatted and laughed, and for this moment life was wonderful. Ma had even made some cinnamon buns for dessert.

৪০ ৫৪

Smita had felt she'd just gone to sleep when she was frightened awake by the terrifying sound of Ma's screams. They came from her parents' bedroom, which was adjacent to the bedroom she shared with her little sister; even though there were four bedrooms in the house, Shruthi did not like sleeping by herself.

Her heart hammering against her ribs, Smita leapt out of bed and ran down the passage. In the parents' room she found Hansaben, the local midwife, standing at the bedside, holding Ma's hand and urging her to be calm. Next to the midwife was a steaming dish of boiling water.

Spotting Smita, Hansaben ordered, 'Go look after your sister. Now.'

'But ... but what's the matter with my Ma?' Smita asked in a tiny voice. She'd never heard her mother make noises like this.

Now wasn't the time for unnecessary questions, the midwife thought; children of today were becoming too inquisitive. 'Your mother is having the baby,' she responded, all business, 'so you just go and stay with your sister and be quiet.'

Although known to be stern with older children, this was un-characteristically dismissive even of Hansaben – but with Subha in agony and things not going as they should, the midwife was deeply concerned. This was different from Subha's previous two births, at both of which she'd assisted.

Smita edged out of the room and went back to check on Shruthi, who was – astonishingly – still fast asleep.

It was a very long night after that, with Ma's continual screaming, which finally died down to moaning as the weak morning sun began lightening the curtains at the bedroom window. Smita, tucked up in her bed with the bedclothes pulled up to her ears, tried to block out the sounds and resolved not to have babies if this was the agony they caused. In the midst of it all, she'd heard Pitaji call the doctor on the phone, pleading with him to come and see to Ma.

She was still awake when Shruthi finally opened her eyes, and the two sisters cautiously made their way into the kitchen, where Pitaji sat, looking worried.

'Is Ma okay, Pitaji?' asked Smita.

'I want Ma,' wailed Shruthi. 'I want num-nums.'

'Ma is sick today, Shruthi,' Shankar said, wiping a weary hand across his forehead and smiling weakly at his girls. 'Your sister will feed you. Now, be a good girl and please try not to be too noisy.'

Smita realised that she would have extra responsibilities today, regardless of how tired she was after almost a full night of no sleep, and she grimly set about buttering some bread and pouring tea for her little sister.

'I want Ma,' Shruthi insisted, tearfully, ignoring the food Smita put in front of her.

Her father lifted her up onto his knee and fed her some bread. 'If you eat nicely, we can see Ma now, okay?'

That seemed to do the trick.

Smita left Shruthi with her father and went back to their bedroom to get their two little stuffed ragdolls. The doll with the brown woollen hair was called Mary-Mary-Quite-Contrary and the one with the yellow hair was Goldilocks. Ma had made them from the offcuts of material she used for sewing the girls' dresses, and they were bright and colourful, with huge hand-painted eyes and rosy mouths. Many other little girls who came to visit were envious of these dolls as their mothers weren't as creative as Subha.

Smita handed Goldilocks to Shruthi and sat down at the kitchen table hugging Mary to her chest, burying her cheek in the mass of wool. Although they were a bit faded, they still were beautiful to the girls and, soft and cuddly, a source of comfort.

After some time, Hansaben came in and told their father that the doctor wanted to see him.

Smita followed the two adults silently, with Shruthi tiptoeing alongside her, tightly holding her hand. Smita knew the grown-ups would notice the two little girls if they went into the bedroom, so she and Shruthi crouched quietly in the hallway outside the bedroom door and strained to hear the conversation between their father and the doctor.

'Congratulations, Mr Maharaj, your twin boys are healthy little babies! They're a bit on the small side, as they arrived early, but they should get stronger by the day. Your wife is weak, however, as there was a lot of blood loss. They all need rest, and I will check up on them in a few days. If there are any other problems, please let me know.'

ॐ ⳤ

While Ma recovered slowly, confined to bed and concentrating on looking after the two tiny little boys she'd produced, Shanti, Shankar's elderly mother, stayed with the family to help with the daily cooking and care of the two girls. Martha got on, as usual, with the general cleaning, although Subha wouldn't have approved of some of the shortcuts she took now that she was relieved, even if only temporarily, of being under the gimlet eye of the mistress of the house.

Smita loved her Dadi, who lived up to her name – shanti meant 'peace' in Hindi. Tranquillity and calm seemed to radiate from her, and this image was augmented by her white widow's sari. She had a cheery disposition, with eyes that seemed to twinkle when she smiled. Plump yet petite, she left a trace of the jasmine scent she dabbed on herself every day when she left the room. Her skin was smooth and brown, like the caramel toffees that she loved to spoil her two little granddaughters with.

Shanti had married Shankar's father, Lal – Dada – in India when she was just sixteen years old. Dadi told the girls a lot about that country, and about how cruel droughts had shrivelled crops in the fields, and how tireless machines had robbed skilled artisans with generations of experience in their bloodlines of their means to feed their families. She spoke about hungry children, and about strong young men who couldn't find work, and who ended up empty-eyed, sitting purposelessly outside their humble family homes.

And she told them about the weeks-long journey she and their grandfather had made on the ship to South Africa, in search of a better life. She told them about the special friends she'd made on board the ship, and how the women would all sit together, picking the stones out of the rice, and chatting in a variety of languages. She spoke about the endless days that seemed to all roll into one, and about the sea that stretched out on all sides to the horizon, where it met the overarching sky, as if the ship and all it held were in a giant blue ball. She told them about sunrises and sunsets, and about the musical instrument they sometimes played on the deck, and about the songs they sang and the games they played, and about the hopes they all had for their new life in the new country. It all seemed incredibly brave and romantic to Smita.

Since Dada had passed on from a sudden heart attack ten years before, Dadi had divided her time between her two sons' homes, as they thought it was not safe for her to live alone. Dadi secretly preferred to live with Shankar, as it pained her to see how her elder son, Krish, had squandered her husband's taxi business and inheritance. Krish's wife, Devi, also pampered their sons, Karan and Kamal, so their behaviour was atrocious at times. She would never say as much, but she far preferred Shankar's girls.

Her and Lal's only daughter, Mala, had been married young and now lived in Durban, too far away to visit often. And Dadi could not stay with her on any terms other than as a temporary guest, as it was considered taboo to live with a daughter after she married.

On this warm winter day, Dadi packed their lunch – dhal and rice – into little steel bowls, then asked Smita to help carry her charpoy and cushion outside. She and her two granddaughters settled down under the bare branches of the peach tree to have their meal and listen to Dadi's wonderful stories while they ate. These were memories that Smita would cherish all her life as rare moments of peace and escape. Under the peach tree, therefore, became a place that she would gravitate to when seeking solace from the trials and tribulations of life. Although the peach tree was a soothing place of consolation year round, the best times were in spring, when it had beautiful pink blossoms, which she and Shruthi would pluck to adorn their hair and pretend to be brides or actresses; and, of course, in summer, when the tree was in full leaf and the fruit ripened, and the sisters could gobble peaches to their hearts' content.

When they had finished eating their lunch, the girls sat quietly while Dadi dozed off, surrendering to the soporific effects of the meal and the wonderful warmth of the midwinter sunshine. But Dadi didn't always sleep when they sat together out here; sometimes she would stare into the distance with unfocused eyes, and Smita would see that there was a sorrow in her face, and she would wonder about it. Once, when she asked Dadi what she was sad about, the old lady said, 'Some stories are best left untold,' and Smita didn't know exactly what she meant by that. Smita found that grown-ups often said things she didn't really understand.

The comforting aroma of frankincense suffused the house daily when Dadi helped Ma and the babies with their bath. On the third day, a herbal infusion of gumtree and syringa leaves was added to the water, to help the convalescing mother to heal.

The babies, however, weren't thriving, and the doctor was summoned once again. He took a long time to arrive, and by the time he did, the two tiny boys were struggling to breathe; both their skins had taken on an alarmingly bluish hue.

The doctor spent a long time behind the closed bedroom door with Ma and the twins. Finally, he came into the kitchen, where the family sat waiting worriedly, with some very grave news. The twin boys, he said, both suffered from a heart defect that couldn't be cured. There was nothing more to be done.

Two days later, the babies died within hours of each other.

Shankar's expression revealed him to be a broken man; he took refuge in his teaching job, disappearing early each day and not returning until early evening. Ma retreated to her room, not talking to anyone and refusing to eat.

Shruthi was especially traumatised; she simply didn't understand and asked constantly where the babas were and asked for Ma. Smita had to undertake the task of caring for her.

Dadi, whose time was taken up caring for Ma and keeping the household running, told Smita, 'When a mother loses a child, it is the greatest grief that a person can endure.' Seeing Smita's confused countenance, she added that Smita would understand when she had her own children – something Smita had already decided against, anyway, after the screams and moans of pain she'd heard during the night her mother had given birth.

Smita was sad for Ma and the babies as well, but the truth was that she couldn't fully understand Ma's inconsolable state. Ma still had Shruthi and her, after all. And all she really wanted was for the winter holiday to end, so she could go back to school and play with her friends. She longed to return to the familiar orderliness of her classroom and Miss Simon, her teacher. She smelt so nice and was so sweet. She was always so elegantly dressed and spoke with perfect eloquence. With her manicured nails, fashionable stockings and high heels, she was the envy of all the girls at school.

Ma was, however, not very complimentary about Miss Simon: 'That woman is too flashy. If that is what education does to you, I am glad my parents did not send me to high school!'

Smita was hurt by these comments: she loved Miss Simon and aspired to be just like her. Smita was determined that she would also be that teacher for whom all the girls would scramble to get the opportunity to carry her fancy satchel to the classroom. She would carry her lipstick in a small bag, just like Miss Simon, and apply it with the aid of a cute little mirror, and, of course, spray tons of perfume all over. Ma had a few bottles of perfume, but Smita was expressly ordered never to touch them or there would be trouble. And somehow Miss Simon's smelt better than the ones Ma had.

She did notice, though, that Miss Simon was always alone at school, and that the other woman teachers seemed to regard her with disdain. They were probably all envious of her, as none of them was as attractive or carried themselves so well.

The male teachers reacted differently: they seemed to be always paying attention to Miss Simon and were also always looking at her.

There were four other female members of staff, but they were old spinsters who were very strict and hardly ever smiled. Two were the teachers for the junior grades, one was the home-economics and needlework teacher, and the fourth was the physical-education teacher, who was very fussy about their hair being neatly tied back with the correctly coloured navy-blue or black ribbons.

A stream of visitors beat a path to the front door of the Maharaj home in Second Street to sympathise with her parents at the loss of their first sons. Fortunately, the house was one of the largest in the area and roomy enough to accommodate many people.

The women who were closer to Ma went directly to the kitchen, where they helped to tidy up, and some would venture into the main bedroom. They brought food for the family, including dokhla, a steamed spicy cake made from cream of wheat and corn, liberally flavoured with green chillies, and other side dishes or pickles or chutneys, as they knew the family would observe a ten-day period of eating food that was only boiled, not fried – it was believed not only that boiled meals would calm the mind, body and soul of the mourners, but also that the bereft family would not enjoy the usual pleasures of life so it would not matter that the food was not so flavoursome.

The other women usually sat in the lounge or the dining room at the front of the house. The men tended to linger on the large front stoep, where they stood smoking or chatting, or in the little front garden.

Sometimes Ma would emerge from her room to greet the visitors, but often she asked Smita to tell them that she wasn't well and was sleeping. Smita wasn't stretching the truth in these cases: Subha had sunk into a deep depression and very often sought solace in the sedating effects of the painkillers she'd been prescribed after the difficult birth of the babies.

Smita's escape was mainly to the little back yard, where she and Shruthi sat under the peach tree, having picnics and playing house with their ragdolls. Occasionally Smita would allow Shruthi to practise her childish version of writing her letters in the sand. Smita pretended to be the teacher, wielding a spindly branch in pretend-admonishment if the work was shoddy.

Smita also would tell her little sister stories from the Ramayana, or the Krishna stories that the little girl loved but barely understood. It didn't matter: Shruthi adored her elder sister and loved to be part of these games that made her feel like a big girl, and distracted her from the upsetting and confusing events that were unfolding indoors.

1955: A visit to Natal

The midwinter school holidays had finally arrived. Now Smita could lie in late, and only venture out when Martha had lit the coal stove so that the kitchen was warm and toasty.

In summer the family spent a lot of the time on the sun-drenched front stoep with its latticed screens to protect them from the harsh midday rays, but in winter the kitchen was the epicentre of the house. Smita did her homework at the big kitchen table while Shruthi played underneath it, and sometimes Ma gave Smita lessons in embroidery and crocheting here. Towards evening, the girls would help with food prep, before the family gathered around for supper.

It was also in the kitchen that Martha helped Ma to fill the big enamel tub with water heated in pots on the stove to wash their faces, as there was no geyser and the water in the taps was freezing cold.

After the morning ablutions, the girls had a steaming cup of tea with spices and aromatic dried-lemongrass leaves, and jam or honey on toast. Presently, the clippity-clop of the horse and cart that brought the weekly delivery from the dairy could be heard, and Smita hurried to bring in the four bottles of milk and one pot of yoghurt that was Ma's normal order. She had to make two trips as there were too many containers to carry at once.

In summer, the family ate dollops of yoghurt with sugar or fresh mint, or with diced cucumber and powdered cumin added to make a delicious relish. However, in winter Ma cooked a mouthwatering dish called khuri-kitchri, which was yoghurt with spices, fried onion, peanuts and chickpea flour, and cumin- and chilli-flavoured rice.

This morning, Pitaji strode into the kitchen, a big smile on his face. 'We're going to visit Ma's family in Natal!' he announced to the girls and laughed when they squealed in delight.

Smita was thrilled: Durban was always warmer than Johannesburg in winter, and she would finally see all her cousins again. Their last trip had been ages ago, as Ma hadn't wanted to travel last winter, as it was too close to her confinement, and in December she was still too depressed.

Smita ran down the hallway and into her parents' room. 'Ma! Ma! We're going to Durban!' she shouted happily.

Subha pushed herself up onto one elbow and regarded her daughter thoughtfully with eyes still bleary from sleep. Then, suddenly, she shot upright and said, 'Come here, my daughter.'

Smita looked worriedly at her mother – she knew that tone of voice and that it didn't mean anything good. But she stepped closer to the bedside, and her mother pointed at the dress she was wearing.

'Do you have no shame, running around like that? If there is a strong wind, can you imagine what will happen? Do you want everyone to see what colour your underwear is? So disgraceful!'

The length of Smita's dresses had indeed got shorter as her height had accelerated, and the hemline of the old dress she was wearing was mid-thigh. She looked at her mother with tears in her eyes and said, 'But Ma, I don't have any longer ones. They are all too short now, but I was scared to tell you.'

Her mother leant forward and caught her daughter in her arms,

27

then crushed her in a completely uncharacteristic hug. 'Oh, my dear, I am so sorry. I have not been a very good mother, have I?' Before Smita could answer, Subha added, 'Go and get your father and tell him that we need to go to town now!'

Smita gaped at her. 'But, Ma, he is having his tea.'

'I don't care what he is doing. My daughters cannot go around looking like urchins! We are getting you some new clothes today. I have not had the energy to sew but we can definitely go shopping.'

Shankar was only too pleased to chauffeur his wife and children into Springs, to the sales at the town shops, as he hadn't seen his wife this invigorated since the death of their baby boys. Subha, smiling and chatting for the first time in almost a year, carefully selected for her daughter the best items from one of the store's bargain boxes – a canary-yellow dress with white polka dots, a pink dress with a huge satin red bow, a baby-blue dress with embroidered flowers, and, Smita's favourite, a peach dress embellished with lace around the hem.

Shruthi, whose main wardrobe consisted of hand-me-downs from her elder sister, also got a few new outfits, so she was happy too.

Subha treated herself to a new cardigan and scarf, as her daily dress was still her saris, of which she had a substantial collection.

The preparations for the trip included making plenty of food, some to take in the car, and some to distribute to the family in Natal as gifts. The girls helped Subha make yummy snacks from the new recipes she'd learnt from her Gujarati neighbours, who hailed from a big state on the western coast of India. Indian cuisine was as diverse as the people who inhabited the country, and every region had different delicacies which were often dictated by the dominant grains, vegetation and spices available. Being curious as well as inventive, Subha hadn't hesitated to adopt some of the exotic-sounding meals that the Gujarati ladies prepared.

The girls also helped Subha bake a huge fruit cake and biscuits to give to all the houses they visited – you couldn't go visiting empty-handed, Ma always said.

Ma made sure she packed all the girls' new clothes, to impress their cousins and as a demonstration of their prosperity, and Shankar loaded the capacious boot of the blue and white Chevy. He was proud of this car with its winged back fenders, fancy headlights and steel grille at the front. It was the envy of most the residents of Bakerton, and of the family's relatives who were not affluent enough to own their own cars.

Ma added some blankets and pillows to the back seat for the girls to nap comfortably. Ma really did think of everything, mused Smita.

The family was finally ready to set off, but first they had to go to the police station to get clearance for the trip – mandatory for 'non-whites' who wanted to travel out of the province. 'Why do we have to get permission from the police to visit our own family, Pitaji?' Smita asked. She was aware that the police generally apprehended bad guys and crooks, so what did Pitaji do that was so bad?

Shankar grimaced. 'Always asking questions, my brown-eyed girl. There are many things that non-whites in South Africa are subjected to, but we Indians are more fortunate than other non-whites in certain respects,' he explained, quite formally. 'For instance, if it was not for Mr Gandhi, the great soul Mahatma, Indians in the Transvaal would still have to be carrying passes around.'

Smita had heard her father speak of the Mahatma several times but she didn't really understand what he was saying – what were passes? Why did other non-whites have to carry them? But she smiled and nodded, grateful to her father for having given her what felt like a grown-up history lesson.

At the police station, the attitude of the white police officers was so derogatory, and Pitaji so obsequious, that it irritated Smita despite her young age. She could not understand why her normally imposing father would suddenly become so docile. Irritably, she allowed her thumb to be inked and pressed down on a form – she was too young to sign her name – and watched as the police helped her little sister do the same.

$$\mathcal{SO}\ \mathcal{CR}$$

Initially, the trip was exciting. The girls stared out the windows at the passing windmills on the farms, spotted cows and horses grazing at the roadside, and tried to identify models of cars that sporadically appeared on the long stretches of road. But soon the dull winter landscape became monotonous and the space in the car felt cramped and confining. It would have been much better to be playing the new card game she'd learnt with her best friends Kala and Nemo from across the road, Smita thought.

In winter, she and her friends were often forbidden from playing outside due to the chilly conditions that prevailed on some days, so they had to be innovative and play indoor games. Now, getting too old to play house and pretend to be mothers with stuffed pieces of material serving for baby dolls, they preferred playing dress-up. This often happened at Smita's house and was lots of fun. Subha had given Smita a few of her older sparkly saris and some costume jewellery, so the girls pretended to be the glamorous Indian actresses they saw at the rare screenings of Indian films at the community hall.

There had been an application made to the Springs town council for the erection of a cinema for the entertainment of the Indian people on an open stand in Bakerton, but this had been denied by the town councillors, many of whom were still opposed to the establishment of an Indian area near Springs at all and wished the Indians would move elsewhere. This would be an ongoing dispute for many years, as some of the other town councillors acknowledged the contribution to the economy from the Indian community.

In the meantime, in the absence of a formal cinema, one of the rich men in the neighbourhood who owned a projector and would sometimes manage to get his hands on Hindi films, would invite his friends and their families from the local community to watch. It was the songs that were mandatory in these movies that the girls would reproduce in their games, and since Smita had the sweetest voice and a talent for recalling the difficult Hindi lyrics, she got to wear the best of the saris and was usually cast as the leading lady. She loved those games.

The family stopped in a lay-by to have some of the cheese-and-tomato sandwiches that Ma had prepared that morning, and hot tea from the thermos, which tasted very much like the plastic cups they drank from. They sat in the car, because if they got out to sit around one of the cement tables at the roadside picnic spots, the bitterly cold wind from the imposing Drakensberg would cause them to catch a cold, according to Ma. The girls were disappointed that they were not allowed to get out.

Soon they were back on the road, and gradually the drab flatlands of the highveld gave way to rolling green hills. This meant that they had entered the province of Natal, although there was still a long way to go before they reached their final destination, Cato Ridge, where Subha had been born and grown up, and where much of her family still lived. As stunning as the scenery was, the rhythmic sound of the car's wheels on the road, plus the warmth of the car interior, took over, and Subha and her daughters dozed off.

A change in the road surface caused the car to shudder a little, stirring them. They had turned off the highway onto the gravel road to the farm in Cato Ridge. Excitement at the prospect of running around again after seven long hours in the car lifted everyone's spirits and they looked eagerly out the windows. Here, the trees and the grass were a rich green, so the landscape also improved their mood. It was so unlike the cramped little garden they had back home.

They drove past some of the farmworkers' children playing on the road with their homemade cars ingeniously constructed from wire. Smita spotted Amos, the little boy she and her cousins had played with when they'd visited almost two years before. He waved shyly and she tentatively waved back, as she remembered the severe reprimand she'd got from her mother for playing with 'the servants' children'.

She quickly brushed off the uncomfortable memory, though, as she recalled the excitement of tucking their bodies inside old, discarded truck tyres and rolling down the lush green hills, and devouring juicy ripe guavas straight off the tree, and learning to roll bicycle rims with a stick. And – something that was seen as the worst sin of all by her mother – eating mealies fresh from the fields, roasted on the little coal fires prepared by the workers, which her mother thought was 'unhygienic'. Granted, quite often these adventures had unfortunate consequences, such as the time she'd suffered from days of constipation when she'd eaten too many unripe guavas, and the deep tyre-burn she'd got on her soft skin. This had annoyed Ma, and Smita had had to bear the brunt of her scolding: 'You are a decent Indian girl, Smita, not one of these native children! You really must behave better!'

This reverie was interrupted by Ma's joyful shout: 'We're here!' She hadn't sounded so happy for a long time.

Nani, Subha's mother, was waiting for them, and as soon as Subha flung herself into Nani's arms, the floodgates burst open. Subha had contained much of her grief over the past months, as she'd had to resume her duties to Shankar and the girls. But when she finally saw her mother, there was no holding back.

Nani held her youngest daughter firmly and murmured, 'Bhagwan has a reason for doing whatever He did. There will be other babies.'

It was easy to see where Ma got her good looks from. Nani, quite regal in appearance, was in her mid-50s, with skin that was flawless and almost unwrinkled except around her kind eyes. Her hair, tied back in a neat bun, was only grey at the temples. Short and stocky, she had a physical strength acquired by years of the hard work on the farm. Nana, Subha's father, had died some years before, shortly after Subha had married, so Nani had had to take over several of the responsibilities of the farming work to help her sons, who at the time had still been young and inexperienced.

The girls' two aunts, who were Ma's younger brothers' wives, lavished praise on the girls, while their younger cousins looked at them in awe. With their new fashionable clothing and the pretty ribbons in their hair, they resembled a family from the land of gold. Despite the creases in their clothes from the hours in the car, the quality was still very apparent. Their cousins on the farm wore mostly home-sewn clothes.

The aunts also stared enviously at Subha's elaborate gold necklace, made from gold sovereigns strung together.

Smita, overwhelmed by her relatives, was wondering how much more of the gushing she could manage, and her cheeks were sore from all the pinching. 'Ooh, so grown up your girls are, Subha! What are you feeding Smita? She is so tall, like a gumtree. Where will you find such a tall boy to marry her?' Hearing this, Smita wanted the ground to open and swallow her up. She was so far away from marriage, but these people ...!

Pitaji was given the royal treatment as the eldest man present; and being a priest added to his exalted status. He was served first, given a glass of cool homemade lemonade, followed by a piping-hot cup of tea with snacks. His favoured status was also apparent at dinner, where he got first pick of every conceivable vegetable dish that had been prepared, together with dhal roti, rotis filled with pulverised chickpeas, fried breads or puris, fresh pumpkin leaves fried with onions, cauliflower and peas fresh from the farm, green beans that had just been picked that day, jackfruit curry, yam curry, steamed yam leaves filled with batter ...

There was also one of Smita's favourite culinary creations, patha, made from the large leaves of the amadumbi (patha meant 'leaves' in Hindi) and a batter of pea flour and spices. The cleaned leaves were arranged in a circular shape and plastered together with the sticky spicy batter and tamarind paste, then rolled up and steamed, sliced, then deep-fried to produce dark crispy spirals.

And even more delectable were the glorious desserts: rich rice pudding sprinkled with almonds, and cream of wheat pudding, both serving as religious offerings in Nani's prayers to give thanks that her youngest daughter from afar was visiting. Smita gave up counting all the dishes or trying to pronounce some of the Hindi names for them. There was only so much she could eat, anyway.

'Girls, see how Indians use the entire amadumbi plant,' Nani said as they tucked in. 'The leaves are made into patha; the stems are steamed and pan-fried with onions, garlic and chilli, to be eaten as bhaji; the tubers can be boiled, peeled and sprinkled with salt, or peeled and made into a sour tamarind-flavoured curry – the tamarind counteracts the itchiness that eating the root sometimes causes.'

Pitaji chipped in here, sharing knowledge he'd no doubt gleaned from his own mother. 'When the indentured Indians came to South Africa, many of them brought with them seeds of the produce they grew for food – jackfruit, mangoes, moringa and many other condiments and spices.'

Bedtime was quite an adventure, as handheld paraffin lamps, with pretty bases for the fuel tank and glass chimneys to contain the flame, were used to lead everyone to their rooms. Smita imagined that she was being led into Aladdin's cave of treasures. In the room that she and her sisters would share with her parents there were pristine white pillowcases elegantly embroidered with exquisite patterns of flowers and birds, executed in perfect stitches. Smita marvelled at the skill and patience this must have required.

The toilet was outside, at the bottom of the garden, so Ma led a little procession to the crude tin structure before going to bed. Shruthi refused to use this facility, however, and no amount of admonishment from Ma could get her to do so. As she was still little, she was allowed to urinate into a chamber pot, which Ma then emptied into the toilet.

The family stayed in Cato Ridge for only two days, as they had shopping to do for certain spices that Ma preferred to buy in Durban, where they were cheaper, and certain vegetables, like okra, bitter gourd, borlotti beans and fresh peanut in their shells, which were not available in Bakerton. And there were also other relatives to visit.

On the onward journey to Durban, about thirty miles away, Smita thought about how her Durban cousins and those on the farm spoke. They pronounced some words quite strangely and even had completely different words for some things. Cooldrink was 'mindral'; 'chips' weren't the hot chips that Ma sometimes made or were the source of the most delicious of smells that emanated out of the café up the road, but the crisps in packets; and cafés were 'tea rooms'. That was quite hilarious to Smita, as she never saw tea served in these places and they were hardly rooms! And where Smita would say 'sure', her cousins would say a word that sounded to her ears more like 'shore'. People at home also tended to have a bit of an Afrikaans accent and often ended a sentence with 'nè', although Smita and Shruthi didn't speak like this, as their parents didn't.

In Durban, they stayed at Ma's elder sister's sprawling house with its huge garden filled with luscious exotic fruit trees – mangoes, litchis, madonis and guavas, and even custard apples, called Sita phal in Hindi, which translated into 'Sita's fruit tree'. Smita could never get enough of the fruit and loved roaming in the garden, picking and eating it, and wiping her sticky fingers on her dresses. The mangoes' golden juice dripped down her chin as she sucked all the delicious flavour from them, and the rich, dark-purple madonis squirted juice of the same colour. Ma, however, was less impressed – Smita's clothes seemed to have a natural propensity to attract the juice, which left immovable stains.

Ma's Durban sister, Auntie Maya, and her husband, Bridge, had nine children, four sons and five daughters. Her cousins ranged from the eldest brother, Vishnu, who was almost thirty, to Rupa, the youngest daughter, who was eight. (Vishnu had been followed by three girls, and more sons were wanted, so the abundance of children was the result of the cycle of hoping and trying to increase the male progeny.) Rupa was Smita's favourite among all her cousins – she was a skinny, sinewy, plucky little girl who was wise beyond her years due to all the knowledge conferred on her by her elder siblings. Rupa had also been forced to develop a thick skin as well as some physical strength, as she'd had to contend with her elder brothers and often fight for what she wanted. Smita admired these qualities greatly.

Bridge's name was actually Bridgelall, and when Smita asked her father why her uncle had opted for such an odd name when he had a perfectly acceptable Indian one, Pitaji explained, 'Indian people who deal frequently with white people tend to anglicise their name, meaning they make it sound more English. So the longer Indian names, such as Moonsamy, are shortened to Sammy or Moon, and Sid is used for Siddhartha – which is a desecration of the name of the Buddha! – and then there are the nicknames, or home names, such as Baby or Dolly.'

'But why?' Smita persisted.

Her father clicked his tongue in impatience. 'Why westerners can't learn to pronounce Indian names is beyond me,' he said, 'and don't even get me started on the silliness of someone called Auntie Baby or Auntie Dolly.'

Smita knew that 'Dolly' was usually reserved for very pretty girls but sometimes the name was translated into the Hindi form and became 'Goodie', which sounded English but was the Hindi word for 'doll'.

Shankar had warmed up to his theme and continued with his explanation, not noticing that his daughter's concentration was waning. 'Boys might be called Babu or Boya, and there's a boy we know who is called Billi, which is the Hindi word for cat, as he has piercing green eyes. Some of the names have an ugly tone too – if someone is very dark-skinned, they may be called Karpai, from the Tamil word for black, karrupu; or a plump person might be referred to as Motu, which is Hindi for "fat". Those people who are very fair might be referred to as Whitey if they are boys or Gori if they are girls, as gori means a white lady or a fair-skinned lady.'

Fortunately, her father finally seemed as tired of this explanation as Smita was now, and he sent her off to play.

One of the highlights of this visit was the impending proposal of marriage to one of Rupa's elder sisters, Rani. Rupa's father had specifically requested that Subha and Shankar meet with 'the boy's' parents. The suitor hailed from a family of educators, so Bridge wanted to make a good impression and Pitaji could impress them with his credentials.

On the big day, Rupa's elder sisters were all very excited and fussing over Rani, who was to meet her suitor for the first time. They were busy painting her nails and applying subtle amounts of powder to make her skin appear flawless and fairer (even though Smita, standing quietly at the door and peeping in with Rupa by her side, thought she was fair enough). To complete the pretty picture, she was draped in a resplendent olive-coloured sari and adorned with some stunning prices of jewellery.

Smita was enthralled at the transformation of her cousin, who she'd always thought of as a bit too pale and skinny. But here she stood as a beautiful young woman with her gorgeous silky black hair piled up attractively on her head, kohl applied to emphasise her huge brown eyes, and smudges of rouge highlighting her cheekbones. If whoever he was didn't think she was pretty, then he would be a very silly man, thought Smita.

The young man's family arrived in a Morris Minor and brought some trays of sweetmeats and fruit as a goodwill gesture. Rupa and Smita, peering through the balustrades of the balcony, watched excitedly as two portly older men in suits, whom Smita assumed to be the elders of the family, led the procession up to the house.

Looking quite dapper in a crisp white shirt, grey pants and patent-leather shoes was the young man who would be the centre of attention. Smita critically assessed his appearance and decided he would make a good match for her cousin.

At the rear was the mother, carrying a tray laden with sweetmeats and flowers, and a boy not much older than herself, who looked directly up at her and winked. Smita gasped in surprise.

Rupa hadn't noticed – all her attention was on the delicious jalebi she'd spotted on one of the platters, and she was hoping they would get to taste some of it. 'It must be from the sweet shop in Victoria Street,' she told Smita.

'Shh!' Smita hissed. She didn't want them to be discovered sitting on the balcony, or they would be shooed away to play. There was just enough space for their two small bodies to fit next to the sliding door that led off the lounge onto the balcony. The door had been left open to let in the afternoon breeze, so they could not only peer into the room and get a good view of all the activity taking place but could also hear everything that went on.

The party entered the lounge, and all the men shook hands before being seated on one side of the room; the women sat on the other side. There was some small talk by the men while the women waited silently. Then Auntie Maya made a subtle gesture and Rani appeared with a tray of tea, followed by her second sister, who brought in the cups and saucers.

Rani put her palms together and greeted the elders without making any eye contact with her suitor. 'Namaste, Uncle and Auntie. May I pour some tea?'

The tea served, Rani stood quietly to one side, looking at no-one, while there was a lot of mundane adult conversation about the weather, mutual friends and relatives, and the increasing prices of food and commodities. Rupa and Smita, growing bored, were about to creep away down the outside stairs, but then, at another subtle signal from Auntie Maya, Rani left the room as silently as she had entered. After she'd gone, there were subtle looks all round.

'Are you happy, son?' asked one of the portly men, obviously the suitor's father.

'Yes, father, I am very happy,' he murmured, blushing furiously.

'That is wonderful,' said Uncle Bridge to the father, then he turned to the red-cheeked young man. 'Now you may have a few words with my daughter on the balcony, where we can keep an eye on you.' He guffawed.

The tension seemed to finally disappear from the room and there was joviality all around. Auntie Maya gestured to the ladies to go into the kitchen, where they would have their tea and sweet treats with abandon away from the men.

Smita and Rupa scrambled to their feet at this and scuttled down to the garden, where they ran into the winking boy. He was quite rough looking but had beautiful long eyelashes that made him slightly endearing.

He had found a football lying in the garden and tried to impress the girls with his prowess and agility. The girls were quite intrigued, and he invited them to join in, only to mock them for their clumsiness, so they left him to his own devices.

'He boasts too much. I hope for Rani's sake that his elder brother isn't the same,' said Smita, annoyed.

The next day the family went to the beach to splash in the surf despite constant warnings from Ma not to get too close to the water. She greatly revered and feared the sea. Ma would always perform an aarti to show obeisance and implore the goddess of the rivers and seas not to take any of her family away. She took along a little brass plate, placed a camphor stick on it and lit it, then, facing the sea, she turned the tray slowly in a circular motion, muttering some prayers. Only after this would the girls be allowed anywhere near the water.

They also could only go to the seaside in the afternoons, as the sun was too strong in the mornings, and they would get sunburnt if they went too early.

The girls cherished these rare visits to the sea. The ocean had such a majestic appearance, and just being on the seashore with their feet sinking into the wet sand, the sea spray on their faces, was a calming, ethereal experience. Smita felt it was truly magical when the warm water brushed over her feet and the white foam dissipated on the golden sand.

To end their visit, their uncle Bridge decided that they would all go to the bioscope in the Indian section of Durban that night. The main cinema in Durban was reserved for whites; the Avalon was for Indians and coloureds, and screened Indian films. This was quite an affair, as Bridge was generally tight-fisted, so the cousins didn't get much opportunity to go out. But with his first daughter due to be married soon, which was at least one burden off his shoulders, Bridge was in good spirits and willing to splash out a little.

They all dressed impeccably, as if attending a wedding or some other important formal occasion. Ma had made Smita and Shruthi straight-cut embroidered satin dresses with frilled collars, and they had pretty brooches to match, and they were the belles of the evening.

Ma herself had acquired a faux-fur coat with buttons that looked like huge diamonds from the sale at Greatermans, so she also looked stunning, and her sister and her nieces looked on enviously.

They watched the latest Hindi film with Raj Kapoor, who was so handsome. Smita wondered why she never saw any men in South Africa who looked like him. Maybe then she would consider getting married. And if someone serenaded you in a mellifluous voice, as Raj did on the big screen, it wouldn't be difficult to marry him. Of course, it would help to be as beautiful as the actresses on the screen as well, and to have their silken voices too.

The plot of the movie was that the heroine was not of the right social standing for her love interest. Then there was the mandatory song-and-dance routine in the pouring rain with the screen siren's attire clinging to her body. Inevitably, the two lovers circled the trees while lip-syncing the great melodies that were sung by playback singers, after which they were cruelly and tragically torn apart. In the end, there was an melodramatic scene in which the woman decided that life was meaningless without her other half, and it would be better to end it all by performing a dance on shards of glass and bleeding to death from the wounds.

Somehow Indian films and actors managed to create scenes that wrenched your heart and made you sob so enthusiastically that you had to carry a handkerchief with you when you visited the cinema. Although she hadn't watched many western films, they really did not have the same effect, Smita thought. Maybe the empathy was greater when the actors resembled you? Smita could not figure it out.

They left for home early the next morning, refreshed after the holiday. Even Ma had more colour in her cheeks.

However, much later that day, as they neared Johannesburg and the cityscape loomed in on the horizon, the heaviness of the smog that choked the air seemed to descend on the family as well. This was true for everyone except Shankar, who relished the fact that he was now back home, back in his territory, the place where he was respected and loved by the people he served.

ဆာ 3 ର

1958–1959: Another pregnancy

Spring announced itself in grand style, with the sun shining brightly on dewdrops, forming crystalline jewels that glistened on the tiny buds waiting to blossom in the garden and on the little open field across the street from the house. The garden boasted an array of flowers planted by Ma and Pitaji – hollyhocks, roses, hydrangeas and marigolds, which, with the wild plants sprouting everywhere, promised to splash colour across the landscape, and the grass was already acquiring a greenish tinge after the drab brown of winter.

At school, there were blossoms on some of the trees in between the wheat-coloured buildings, breaking the monotony of the rows of prefabs. This transformation made Smita smile with delight in the crisp morning air, and her mood remained positive as she walked home, tearing off her jersey to signify to herself the end of winter.

School had been eventful today, with the commemoration of Arbor Day and the planting of a tree by the head boy and head girl. The principal had made a boring speech, but the highlight of the day was a rendition of 'All Things Bright and Beautiful' by Miss Simon and the few girls who made up the school choir. Smita wasn't allowed to join the choir – Ma had a problem with her singing

Christian hymns – but she maintained that all music was beautiful, and she hummed the tune all the way home.

'Smeets, you're home!' Shruthi shrieked as her big sister walked in the front door. 'You have to hurry up! Ma is going to the doctor today and you have to change, like I did when I came from school. You know Ma does not like us to wear our uniforms after school because we might make them too dirty and they will get stains on them. See, I am wearing my dress that Ma made ...'

Against the background of Shruthi's chattering, Smita's mind raced. Ma had been acting a bit strange lately, and this morning Smita had heard her throwing up. She'd also been sleeping more than usual. Also, and even more unusually, she hadn't made fresh roti for Pitaji's lunch, but instead had used shop-bought bread. For Subha, non-Brahmin people – white or black – couldn't possibly be aware of the standards of hygiene required for food preparation, and certainly couldn't be trusted to produce a hygienic and edible bread; and, anyway, those people ate pork and beef!

Ticking off her mother's symptoms on her fingers, Smita ventured a guess at what the problem with Ma was, and the cause of her 'illness'. The source of this newfound wisdom was the conversation her friend Bindu had had with a group of classmates about why vomiting meant a woman was pregnant. Bindu's very serious theory, which had seemed perfectly plausible to a group of eleven-year-olds, was that the baby needed space to grow in the woman's tummy and the food was constantly getting in the way, so it had to be pushed out. Of course, it was much worse if it was something yucky that the mother had eaten, like brinjal, or any green vegetable, really, Bindu said, wisely. They'd had brinjal for supper the night before; how clever of Bindu, Smita thought; she must remember to tell her if her mother was indeed pregnant!

These days, Smita and her friends were constantly pondering and trying to unravel the great mysteries of life. One of the most common ones was gossiping about who was the latest to be hit by the 'period bug' and the implications of this. It was one of the aspects of growing up that Smita was dreading the most, especially after listening to the horrific tales about the pain and the mess – and that it meant that you were ready to get married. Some of her friends told her that the pain was like getting kicked in the stomach and some even had pain in their back; a few said that it was so bad, no tablet helped – they just had to sit with a hotwater bottle clutched to their tummies and wait it out. Also, the amount of blood could be horrendous, an apparent haemorrhage, accompanied by feelings of weakness.

The entire concept sounded revolting, just like the other changes that were taking over her body without her consent: the unwelcome budding of her breasts, and the fact that she would soon need to wear a brassiere; and the unsightly sprouting of hair in some un-mentionable places. Thank God she'd discussed these anomalies with her friends, otherwise she would have thought she was the victim of some freak disease, like the Elephant Man they'd learnt about in science class.

Saras, one of the quieter girls in her class, had been the first among them to get the period bug. She was a little plumper and more buxom than the other girls, as she was a year older. Her parents had sent her to school a year later than the other girls, as her mother had been ill and she was kept at home to give her company and assist her when possible. Saras's demeanour also made her a little unapproach-able, as she viewed her classmates' games as childish and boring, and was always careful not to muss up her perfectly oiled braid or her perfectly pressed uniform.

Saras hailed from a Tamil-speaking family whose roots were in southern India. Back when they had first arrived in South Africa, most immigrant Indian families of Hindi- and Tamil-speaking origin had found work as vegetable hawkers or railway workers, but Saras's family were traders.

Saras came into school one day, very pleased with herself and sporting beautiful fresh flowers in her hair (which she was promptly made to remove by the teachers). She had not been to school for a few days, so all the other girls were curious, and, although none of them admitted it, envious of the flowers as well.

At the 10 o'clock break, Saras could hardly wait to tell the other girls that she had 'come of age'. Regarding the flowers, Saras explained, 'My granny said we have to do this thing, so the boys and their mothers can know that I will be able to get married. See what presents I got also,' she added, pulling up her sleeve to reveal a stunning gold-filigree bracelet inlaid with red and white gemstones. 'This was my granny's when she came from India. And I also got this,' she said, tugging at her neckline to show off an elegant necklace with a flower-shaped pendant. 'This was from my uncle who has a business.'

The girls all oohed and aahed, but Saras wasn't finished yet. 'I was treated like a princess,' she said.

'My mummy says that people also call it Aunt Susie,' piped up Bindu, who had a problem being quiet and was annoyed at Saras getting all the attention.

'Shh,' chided the other girls, and urged Saras to continue. 'What happened? How did you know?' they asked.

'Well, when it first happened, I had to stay in the house; they wouldn't let me go outside and I was upset. Also, I wasn't allowed to go even close to the place where we have the small brass lamp that we fill with oil every day to pray – you know, the God lamp. My mother said I wasn't clean.' Smita recognised the truth of this; it was her duty to wash her family's brass lamp, as well as the deities housed in the little enclosed alcove next to the lounge reserved for praying, when Ma wasn't 'clean'.

Saras continued, 'I was crying but they gave me a chocolate and crisps and cooldrink, so that made it better. Then Ma said that on the weekend there would be a function for me, and I must choose a sari to wear from her special saris.'

'You get to wear a sari?' asked Smita with wide eyes.

'Yes, and jewellery. But first my aunts and my mother had to do a nalangu on me.'

'A nalang-what?' asked Mariam, one of the Muslim girls in their group.

'The yellow stuff, you know, manja, like when people get married. They put it all over me like a lotion but didn't rub it in. They said it was to clean me. Then I was given an oil bath, like I was a baby, and they dressed me up in this pretty red sari of my mother's, put the flowers in my hair, put the red-coloured powder on my feet and a dot on my forehead, and sang these songs in Tamil and danced and said that I was now ready to be a woman!'

'But you are only twelve!' said Smita, shocked.

'Yes, but when you start having bleeding, you can have babies after that.'

This was too much for all the girls, who were chattering noisily among themselves now.

'Also, they made lots of sweet things and food, and invited all our family and friends to see me.'

By now the girls had information overload and had to discuss this by themselves. They wondered if they would all go through this ceremony.

Mariam said that she knew it wouldn't be so for her, as she was Muslim, and it was definitely considered unclean to have a period – it wasn't anything to be celebrated. When it was Ramadan time, for instance, women did not fast if it was 'their time'. Many variations of their experiences with mothers, cousins and elder sisters followed, until the bell rang again, summoning them to class.

ஐ ௧

Ma and Pitaji returned from the doctor with the news that Ma would be having another baby in March of the following year. The girls were happy enough, as babies were cute, but they were also curious as to how their parents and the doctors knew. Ma did not look like there was a baby in her tummy.

Ma said that there were ways for doctors to tell these things in advance, and when they were older, they would understand better. Smita balked at this as she felt very old today, after being party to all of Saras's stories.

The pregnancy went well, and Subha was in high spirits in spite of the fact that they once again missed their summer trip to Durban as she was advised not to travel. But as the time for the birth came closer, Subha became more and more anxious. Would it be a girl or a boy? She couldn't help hoping for a boy. But she did not want twins again – that pregnancy had been difficult, and she didn't even want to think about the horror of the delivery, never mind what happened afterwards. And if this baby did not survive, what would she do? She could not bear another loss.

She had actually initially been reluctant to fall pregnant again and had tried the old ways of avoiding pregnancy. But finally she had decided that she was ready for this one, as she needed to give Shankar a son.

It suddenly dawned on her in the midst of these thoughts that Smita's birthday was two days away. She decided she would surprise her and bake that delectable-looking chocolate cake that she had seen in last week's newspaper. The women's page was the only section that interested her, and Shankar often saved it for her after he was done reading the rest of the paper.

She remembered that there were some colourful sprinkles left over from Shruthi's birthday, and since it was probably the last childhood birthday for Smita, it would be very appropriate to decorate the cake with these. Adding the finishing touches with the last of the late rose blooms, she felt satisfied with the end result.

Smita was overjoyed when she saw the cake and thrilled to receive her gift of a gold necklace.

For this delivery, Pitaji had said that they would take no chances – it would not be a home birth, and he would take Ma to the hospital when her labour started. But then everything happened so suddenly.

It was an unusually warm day on the first day of March and the girls had just got home from school.

'Smita!' Ma called as they came in the front door.

Smita could hear the edge to her mother's voice, and she ran to where Subha was lying on her bed, her hands clasped over her huge tummy. 'Go with Martha to fetch the midwife,' Ma instructed her.

Smita was in a state of shock. 'Ma! Are you okay? Must I call Pitaji at his school?'

'Just go, child! The midwife must come now. This baby is coming! There is no time to wait for your father,' her mother said, her breath coming in gasps.

Smita, who was terrified by what was happening, was so grateful that Martha was there to help. 'I have two small children, only two years and five years old,' Martha told her as they walked quickly down the road towards the midwife's house. 'I must leave them with my old mother at the homestead in Basutoland. I miss them so much but we need money I am earning here. You know, mos, it is so cold there, much more than here. I need to buy the shoes for them, the jackets, blankets, all costing so much money. At least your mother gives me some old blankets and jerseys so I can send for them.'

Martha chattered on, saying that in her country it snowed in winter, and although it looked beautiful, like an enormous white carpet, the temperatures were freezing. They also had the most amazing mountains that were beautiful, and not like the dry, dreary landscape of the Transvaal, she said.

Back at the house, Hansaben instructed Smita and Martha to prepare everything. In a daze, Smita helped Martha to get the hot water ready, then got the old clean towels out the linen cupboard and made a pile of them. Martha took the water and towels down the passage to Hansaben before silently retreating to the kitchen with Smita and Shruthi to wait.

It didn't take long. There were a few moans from Ma but this was quickly superseded by the piercing cry of a baby. Smita and Shruthi looked at each other in delight – that was the very healthy cry of their new sibling, and so soon!

As if on cue, they heard the front door open and they ran to meet Pitaji to tell him the news in case he did not hear the racket that the baby was making.

Hansaben emerged smiling and, after humbly greeting Pitaji, told him that everything was fine, and he could go and see Subha.

To Subha's obvious dismay, the child was another girl. Within days of the birth, she sank into a deep depression. She did not want her ritual third-day bath, instead asking Hansaben to bath the baby and massage her with the aromatic oils, saying that she was too tired to do it.

Subha knew that she should be more involved with her baby, never mind her two elder daughters, but she just couldn't shake off the feeling of despair. Her new little daughter, Meera, beautiful even though she was slightly darker than the older two, was sweet-natured and compliant, hardly ever crying for no reason. However, she was not the son that Subha had been hoping for, and she just could not find the will to care for her newborn.

The night-time feeding became a chore, and she was exhausted the next day, finding even the simplest of tasks difficult. After the pregnancy and childbirth, plus the disturbed sleep a tiny baby brings, it was normal to be tired, but this was different. It was a weariness and listlessness that made her feel completely fatigued, and it became more and more difficult to emerge from her bedroom. Nothing interested her any more. Visitors came over, bearing beautiful gifts of clothing for the baby, delicious treats that were believed to energise the new mother, and even meals for the family but none of this seemed to alleviate Subha's mood.

She spent more and more time alone, communicating little, and being surly when she did. Matters were not helped by the onset of an unforgiving winter, and as Subha became progressively sadder, she felt more and more helpless and alone – but also had a deep sense of guilt, realising she was failing as a mother.

Subha did less and less in the house, doing the bare minimum for the baby, and leaving Martha and Shankar to pick up the slack, and Smita to care for Shruthi. Shankar finally discussed with his wife the need for help with the cooking, cleaning and other housework, and with caring for the children. To his surprise she did not disagree.

They decided to ask Dadi to come and live with them for an indefinite period, and also to invite Martha to stay overnight for a few days each week, so that she could assist early in the mornings and late in the evenings, and with nighttime feeds for the baby if necessary. The house had two spare bedrooms, so there would be enough space for everyone – the one Martha would use usually served as a store room, and had an outside entrance into the back yard, so she could come and go via the back gate.

Shankar assured his wife that he would permanently lock the inside door of what would be Martha's room, as Subha would not allow a maid to sleep inside the family home; and Martha would use the ramshackle outside toilet in the lean-to in the back yard. Subha was simply following the customs of the time in her country of birth: it was usual, for instance, for employers to have separate crockery and cutlery for 'the girl', as the maid was often called, and Subha kept aside some old plates, bowls and mugs, plus a separate knife, fork and spoon for Martha to use.

Shankar was also aware that he would be providing a necessary excuse for his mother to escape from her other daughter-in-law, with whom she lived but did not have a good relationship. Fortunately, his brother still lived in the Asiatic Bazaar in Germiston so he did not need to travel far to fetch her – it was only about thirty miles to the west.

As he drove into the area, he noticed that the squalor had increased as more people moved in, and there was still no proper sanitation, plumbing or drainage, so the entire place smelled like a sewer. His father's old house was still in good condition but he, Shankar, would not be able to bring himself to live in the midst of this dilapidation and decay.

He was very relieved that his mother was packed and ready, and excited to spend time with her two – now three – granddaughters, so there was no prolonged visit for him there.

෨ 4 ෮

1960: A strange visit with Ma

Barberton, about two hundred miles to the east, had experienced a boom when gold was discovered there in 1874 and in its heyday was quite an economic and social hub. Now, though, the area was famous for its fruit farms, which produced some of the most delicious mangoes, oranges and nuts the country had to offer.

Pitaji's close friend, Uncle Hemant, had seen the opportunity to open up a general dealer in Barberton for the farm workers. He'd sent his son ahead, to set up a home there, so there were prayers to be performed to bless the new house.

The new shop and Barberton were very far away, and Pitaji explained to the girls, as he prepared to leave on the Friday, that he would stay over at his destination for a couple of nights and be back on Sunday. He promised to bring them some of the fruit that grew there, so that they would have something to look forward to.

Dadi was spending some time with her eldest son, Uncle Krishna, in Germiston, and Martha had also taken a few days off, so Subha and the girls were alone. Ma tried to fill the gap created by Pitaji's absence, giving them toasted-cheese sandwiches with hot chocolate for supper rather than the normal Indian fare. She also promised that they would go for a walk early on Sunday morning after a treat of pancakes drizzled with honey. They had to promise Ma that this little excursion would be kept a secret from Pitaji, and she would get them the normally forbidden crisps and Coo-ee cooldrinks if they played along.

It was a beautiful sunny summer's day with clear blue skies and, as it was still early, the sun did not burn down on them as viciously as it would have at midday. Ma bought them the illicit treats, and they made sandwiches with the potato crisps and bread. When these were immersed in the fizzy drinks, the contrasting flavours of the salty crisps with the sweet liquid was sublime.

Baby Meera was fast asleep as Subha pushed her along in her pram. Shruthi's short legs tired quickly, and she asked Smita to give her a 'baleta', as the women on the farm called carrying their babies on their backs. Smita knelt down so her younger sister could scramble up.

Unexpectedly, Ma turned into the less popular and less affluent section of houses where the girls were normally forbidden to venture, and they had to gingerly navigate around puddles of what they hoped was just murky water overflowing from the burst gutters. Shruthi complained of the malodorous scents pervading the air, but Ma told her to be quiet.

As they turned the next corner Smita realised to her horror that this was the witch Kanamma's house that she and her friends often dared each other to go to. Auntie Kanamma had a reputation for practising black magic, and could apparently go into a trance and predict the future, and give blessings to anyone with any particular affliction. Pitaji was extremely critical of her occult practices and scolded many people for visiting her.

In the yard, the offensive street smells were masked by the unmistakable aroma of incense that pleasantly infused Smita's nostrils. There was a brass bell outside alongside a little wooden bench, which was unoccupied, as it was a Sunday, and this was one of the reasons that Subha had chosen to visit on this day. Most people were either resting or visiting relatives, so did not seek counsel on Sundays. From the rumours she'd heard, Saturday was the most popular day.

Auntie Kanamma emerged from the house clad in a bright-orange sari and bangles that clattered when she put her palms together to greet Ma. Smita was surprised at how attractive she was. She had an angular face with high cheekbones and huge bright shiny eyes that smiled as she looked at the children. Smita had expected someone with great protruding yellow teeth, jet-black irises and dishevelled hair but she looked quite majestic and enchanting.

Ma returned the greeting and, before she could stop herself, burst into tears. For Smita, this unabashed display of emotion in the presence of a stranger was shocking but she could sense that this woman had the power to see through you and make you confess any sins that you might have committed and reveal all your deepest and darkest secrets.

'It's alright, Ma. Come inside,' Auntie Kanamma said. 'Leave the children. Lord Siva will protect them here. You just come in and tell me why you came here to see me.' Kanamma put an arm around Subha's shoulders and winked at Smita, motioning that they should sit on the bench. From inside a fold of her sari she produced two lollipops, which she handed over to Smita and Shruthi before ushering Ma into the house.

Smita was disappointed that she wasn't going to be privy to the conversation between the two women, but she realised that if she crept up to the door, she would be able to hear most of what was happening inside. Making sure that Shruthi was occupied with her lollipop and Meera was fast asleep, she quietly approached the doorway and peeped inside. Fortunately, the women were facing away from the door, so they wouldn't see her as long as she remained quiet. Smita watched attentively as the scene unfolded before her.

Subha allowed herself to be comforted for a few moments, as she was tired of not having anyone to share her woes with. After she had calmed down a little, she swore Kanamma to secrecy about this meeting, as Pitaji would be livid if he found out. Kanamma assured the distraught woman that she would never breach the confidentiality of their conversation and that she never divulged the details of her consultations.

Visibly relieved, Subha proceeded to tell Kanamma about her desire to give her husband a male heir but she had a firm belief, she said, that she'd been cursed by her older sister-in-law, who came from a family renowned for strange practices and who was also deeply envious of her. Her sister-in-law's ploy was to inflict this bad luck on her so that her husband's nephews would inherit all the family fortune, including what her husband had acquired over all these years through his own sheer hard work.

Kanamma read Subha's palm, which revealed that she would bear her husband many children. 'Producing a son will be difficult but not impossible,' the witch said, then added, 'I caution you against having sons, my daughter, as they could come with problems.' In truth, Kanamma had little time for Subha's lack of appreciation of girl children, whom she regarded as incarnations of the divine Mother Kali herself.

Subha, operating on a lack of sleep and a surfeit of hope, selectively heard the first bit and didn't hear the second. And, anyway, with all the prayers that she and Shankar had performed … In her own mind, she decided there and then that she would rear her sons to be fine upstanding men. However, as a precautionary measure, she asked if Kanamma would be able to influence this with her powers, to speed up the process of producing male progeny, as three daughters were surely enough?

Kanamma said that she needed to meditate to invoke the powers of the goddess Kali, who influenced matters of fertility. The witch then turned to face the little shrine furnished with figurines of the gods and goddesses; a low table was draped in a splendid red cloth with gold sequins that sparkled in the light shed by the oil lamps that burned at the feet of the deities. *But this isn't witchcraft!* Smita thought, looking at the scene, which was reminiscent of her own parents' prayer room, except a lot prettier.

When Kanamma emerge from her meditative state, she instructed Subha that the goddess Kali wanted a sacrifice of a black rooster so that a son could be born. 'The blood shed from the rooster means that no unnecessary blood will be shed from your son,' Kanamma concluded.

On hearing this, Subha cringed: the family adhered to a strict vegetarian diet. But she wasn't surprised: it made sense that you needed to perform a sacrifice for a male, as there had to be a raw demonstration of power.

Shankar would be disgusted by this, she knew, but he didn't know everything, especially when it came to female matters.

Kanamma was still talking to her, saying that this must be done on a Monday, and Subha's mind was racing as to how she could conceal all this from her husband. But then she realised that in fact a Monday would be perfect as her entire family would be in school – her husband teaching and her daughters in class. 'Can I come next Monday?' she asked Kanamma.

The witch agreed, and Subha thought happily to herself that all her prayers would soon be answered, and in time her daughters would all be married off to wealthy suitors, and her sons would look after her in her old age.

Smita, listening as still as a statue at the door, was horrified. She knew, of course, that many people ate meat, and that on the farm they did kill some of the chickens for eating, but this was always done by the servants and they were never allowed to watch. Moreover, she distinctly recalled listening to a conversation in which Pitaji had vehemently condemned the practice of sacrifice, saying that real priests did not condone it any more. His father, whose ancestors were the learned Brahmin priests of India, had told him so.

Smita shuddered. What would Pitaji do if he found out about all of this? Why was her mother resorting to this? Smita knew that Ma badly wanted a son – but to the extent of performing sacrifices and who knew what else?

However, when Smita saw her mother's face as she stepped out of the house, the calm, satisfied expression and radiance that seemed to envelop her, she thought that maybe it would be worth it.

ℬ 5 ℜ

1962: Dadi's sadness

Smita woke to the chattering of women. She stumbled out of bed, wondering what was going on, then remembered that Ma was hosting the papad-making this year. Smita's family was often given honorary status within the community due to the fact that Pitaji conducted the pujas for the families, so the women of the community were always willing to come and help Subha.

Papad was a spiced condiment that spruced up any meal and was a necessary addition to the otherwise mundane lunchtime offering of lentils and rice, and compensated for the lack in variety of vegetables available in the Transvaal. As Pitaji had told them before, the indentured labourers who had landed in Natal in the late 1800s and early 1900s had brought the seeds of the vegetables that were common fare in Indian cuisine, and most of these labourers had hailed from farms in India and knew how to cultivate vegetables. But as most of the Indians who had moved up to the north of the country were traders, they did not consider husbandry in any form, not to mention that the climate in the Transvaal was not conducive to growing these foodstuffs, so they had to rely on the rare deliveries of vegetables from Natal.

The women from the community generally met once a year to

make tons of papad, which they would distribute among themselves. It really was fun, as in addition to getting to assist with the rolling of the dough and ferrying the rolled papad into the hot sun to dry, many of the women brought their daughters with them to help, so Smita would have lots of friends.

The community effort was required because it was quite a mammoth task, as they made huge quantities and the work had to start early. The papad needed time to dry, and summer afternoons often brought thunderstorms, so they had to shape the dough before any typical summer-afternoon shower ruined all their hard labour.

For the rice papad, the dough had to be prepared with rice flour, chillies, sesame seeds, thymol seeds and cumin seeds, and then steamed before it was rolled out and set out to dry. For the urad-dhal papad, the prepared dough would be kept overnight in a cool spot in the pantry before it was rolled out and left to dry. In the olden days, when black gram flour wasn't freely available, the pulses had to be tracked down and purchased, and then pulverised to make the flour, before work could begin on the urad-dhal papad.

Smita, like most children, preferred the rice papad with its fluffy, crunchy texture and airy quality, almost like an Indian version of shop-bought crisps. Rice papad also complemented certain desserts, its pungent salty flavours somehow enhancing the rich, sweet milky taste of kheer and seviyan.

After Smita had assisted Shruthi and baby Meera with their morning ablutions, the three sisters ventured shyly into the kitchen, where seven women were chatting merrily over tea and eats they'd brought along, while a huge pot of some glorious-smelling food bubbled away on the stove. Yes, there was work to be done, but lunch had to be prepared for the troops.

The women all gushed over Meera. 'Oh my, Subha, what a cutie this little one is! So chubby, with red, rosy cheeks.' 'And such curly, soft hair. You must have been eating a lot of spinach during the pregnancy for her hair to be like that.' 'All your girls are so lovely.

Look at Smita, she is just too beautiful. So tall and fair and slim. Just like one of the movie stars! You are very lucky.'

Smita blushed at all this attention and asked Subha if they could go for a walk as it was such a sunny day. Unfortunately, this was within earshot of their busybody neighbour. 'Oh, you can't let the girls go in the sun, Subha – they will get all burnt and dark. Smita is so lucky, she is a bit fair now. What if she gets so sunburnt that no one will want to marry her?'

'Oh well, at least my daughters are pretty, like everyone says, and they will not have a problem with finding a husband,' Subha said, offhandedly.

Smita was surprised at this remark, as Subha rarely complimented her daughters, but she also knew that the comment was to keep up the façade of being completely blissful with her life and not admitting that she had any problems.

Three little tables were set up in the small back yard and the seven women, armed with flat silver thalis and rolling pins, gathered around them. The dough had been prepared by Subha already, and each table was allocated their portion. Then the women began churning out thin, perfectly round discs of papad, while Smita and Shruthi collected the finished product and set them to dry on trays strategically placed on the front veranda to capture the maximum amount of sun.

The teams had finished by midday and broke for lunch, after which, to Smita's delight, Subha allowed her to try her hand at rolling a few papads with some of the leftover dough. Ma showed her that papad needs to be rolled very thinly, so you needed to apply a lot of pressure when rolling – unlike for roti, which required little pressure, as if it was too thin you'd end up with hard, crisp rotis, which nobody wanted. 'You should be able to see through the disc when it's finished,' said Ma, holding up a disc she'd rolled and cut to show Smita.

As Smita pulled a piece of dough towards her prepared to roll it out, her mother sighed heavily beside her. 'I don't know why I'm so tired and breathless,' she said.

'Maybe you're having another baby?' Smita suggested.

'Well, that is what you get for showing gratitude to your husband sometimes at the wrong time of the month,' Subha murmured.

Smita felt her cheeks burning and recalled the whispered conversations she had had with her friends about this and how it all seemed completely disgusting to them; they concluded that men or boys enjoyed this horrendous act more than women. Then there was 'the talk' by the science teacher, who discussed 'human reproduction' with a class of all girls in such boring biological terms that it was over before they could begin to get a proper grasp of what they were being told – followed by a dire warning that they were never to do these things until they were married, which naturally led them to not desiring ever to be married.

Smita was hoping to hear more detail from her mother, as sometimes the information she got from her friends was a little dubious. 'What you mean, Ma?' she asked, feigning confusion. 'If you are nice to your husband, do you have babies?'

Subha laughed but didn't answer the question. 'I'm going inside to sleep. Please keep an eye on the papad and wake me if there is a storm coming.'

Smita went over to sit under the peach tree with Dadi, who was busy crocheting while keeping an eye on Meera, who was sleeping peacefully. When she saw her eldest granddaughter approaching, she put down her crochet hook and held a finger to her lips, indicating that Smita should keep her voice down.

'You can massage my old bones while I tell you some stories,' Dadi said quietly, handing Smita her tin of balm.

Smita gladly opened the tin that contained Dadi's own concoction of eucalyptus oil, olive oil and Sloan's liniment. Smita thought that just the smell made you feel better sometimes.

She settled next to her granny, taking one of her arms and rubbing a bit of balm into it, not forgetting to check if there were any grey clouds approaching, while Dadi closed her eyes and began to speak.

'I am getting old now, Beti, and I need to tell something so you will know where you come from. I can't tell your mother, as she has her head too much in the clouds, and it is too embarrassing for me to tell your Pitaji, as we do not discuss these things with men. What you will find out will shock you, but as I said, I have to share this burden that I have carried with me for so many years.'

Smita, noticing Dadi's eyes fill with tears, was intrigued.

'Your Pitaji's father, your Dada, fell in love with me, and accepted a meagre sum as a dowry. But his parents never forgave me for not contributing to their fortunes. When Lal tired of the abuse, he decided to make his fortune far away from the petty bickering over what he thought were archaic practices that did not make sense. It was very modern thinking for an Indian man, but I was thankful for it, as it gave your Dada and me a new beginning and a new life. You must find a man who will defend your honour Smita, someone who will stand up for you, love you for everything that you are and not just your pretty face. Remember that, Beti.'

Dadi waited for Smita to nod her acknowledgement before continuing. 'I was very heartsore to leave India and my family, who I knew I would never see again, but I had to follow my husband's wishes.

'Although when you were younger, I told you only the adventurous side of the trip, it was actually terrible. We were paying passengers, not labourers, but the officers and crew still considered us as less than human and often abused us. Our cabin was below deck in steerage class and very close to the hold where the labourers, who were called "indentured", were kept in cramped, unhygienic conditions. And although there were latrines on board, women tried to avoid using them because of the harassment there, from the crew and other men. Dada used to accompany me when I needed to go.

'Due to the storms and the squalls at sea, almost everyone got seasick sooner or later. Your grandfather, God bless his soul, had a much weaker disposition than I did and got seasick very early on in the journey. So I had to care for him and clean up the vomit every day, in addition to trying to keep the baby, your uncle Krishna, well and keep up my strength. And our lodging area was often filled with the stench of the unemptied faeces and urine buckets, vomit and human sweat. Illnesses and infections were easily spread because of the crowded conditions on board.'

Dadi glanced down at Smita, who had long since stopped massaging her grandmother's arm, and was simply holding both her hands in hers. 'Anyway, that is just the start of my very sad story and I cannot carry on now. But I have begun writing it down, and you, as my favourite and most intelligent grandchild, will read it one day.'

Smita watched as Dadi lowered her head and the tears fell onto their clasped hands. 'I had to pay the price for the life of Dada and my baby,' Dadi whispered.

'What do you mean, Dadi? Why are you crying?' asked a bewildered and concerned Smita. Dadi's stories were mostly fun ones about growing up in India, and then about life with her three rambunctious children. This wasn't like her at all.

The two sat in silence for a while, then Dadi said softly, 'I have not shared this story with another soul, but in the twilight of my life, I need someone else to know my story. Please do not repeat a word of this. In time, you will learn everything, and I trust you to decide what you will do with the story.'

Dadi looked up at Smita and smiled through her tears. Gently, she disentangled her hands from Smita's. 'See, I am getting carried away now and rambling on like the old woman I am. Look now, the storm is coming. Run and tell your mother.'

೫೦ ೧೩

Only a few weeks after this conversation, Dadi's health deteriorated rapidly. She complained of pains in her throat and mouth and increasing difficulty swallowing. She said that she recalled a similar affliction had caused the demise of her own grandmother, and often would tell Smita that her 'time had come'.

It pained Smita greatly to see her beloved Dadi suffering – and physically diminishing before her eyes, as her inability to eat caused her cheekbones to protrude and her shoulder bones to stick out sharply. Within a short time, her clothes hung on her emaciated frame and the usual happy glint in her eyes disappeared. It was deeply unsettling to see Dadi so lifeless and immobile.

The doctors confirmed the family's fears: Dadi had cancer and there was nothing more that could be done for her.

Cancer of the throat and mouth was a condition that claimed the lives of many women of Indian origin. The cause baffled the medical profession at first, but finally it was discovered that the culprit was the small, innocuous-looking seed of the areca palm, known as betel nut. These seeds, dried and broken into edible little pieces, were used as a cure for worm infestations, to prevent halitosis and as a digestive. For centuries, people from the Indian subcontinent had enjoyed this treat after their meals, often mixing the betel nut with fennel seeds, and occasionally with dried coconut or little bits of candy, without realising the health hazards of this practice.

Dadi was aware of her illness and the prognosis, and Smita saw the sadness in her eyes when she spoke of why her eldest son wouldn't visit her more often. 'After everything I went through for him, he treats me like this!' she said, angrily. 'He was a difficult child, always rebellious, and it was difficult for us to teach him – so unlike your father, Smita, who took to the holy books like a duck to water. That is why he is so calm: he has true faith in what he does. He doesn't do it just to make money, which the Gods and the people are both sensitive to.'

She'd brought up her sons to respect women and treat them as equals, she told Smita, something that did not always seem to have positive results, as both her sons seemed to be dominated by their wives. 'Children! After you take care of them and grow them into men and women, they marry, and they want to lead their own lives and abandon you to a lonely existence, remembering you only on Diwali and your birthday, if they remember you at all. My daughter, Mala, has also forgotten me after her marriage.' The old lady shook her head. 'Well, at least your Pitaji cares for me.'

After these conversations, Dadi would end up out of breath and fall into a deep slumber chanting, 'Ram nam satya he,' 'God's name is truth,' which is what the great Mahatma Gandhi said just before he died.

As Dadi's health deteriorated further, Smita cared for her as she would have for her baby sister, often spooning pulverised lentils or mashed vegetables into her mouth. Dadi was unable to tolerate any spices, so Ma or Pitaji prepared special foods for her. The doctor had prescribed a high dose of morphine syrup, so Dadi frequently seemed delusional, muttering about the reunion she looked forward to with her beloved Dada, and recollections of her childhood in India, and of her parents' struggle to pay the dowries for their three daughters.

In her grandmother's final days, the children weren't allowed to see her – she was suffering too much, and in too much pain, said Pitaji, who cared for her almost single-handed.

Early one morning, when the late April chill was seeping through the gaps in the windowpanes and declaring its presence, Pitaji told them that Dadi had finally departed this life. It was very difficult for Smita to grasp that her granny would never awake and that she would not see her again. She heard the adults say that she was in a better place and would have no more suffering.

Smita felt deeply miserable. She would really miss Dadi, their chats under the peach tree, her affectionate soothing massages when Smita felt under the weather, and her calming presence in the house.

Her mother did not scold them or get upset as much when her granny was there.

At the funeral, Smita saw the peaceful look on Dadi's face, so maybe she *was* in a better place now. But looking at her immobile, frozen form was so difficult and she could not stop the tears and the wrenching feeling in her chest. She sobbed until it was time for the body to be taken to the crematorium where tradition dictated that women and children were forbidden to attend.

The next few days were filled with the planning for the mandatory religious ceremonies that followed.

Smita often had errands to run and little jobs to do in between the constant babysitting of her two younger sisters. The three were forming a close bond, and her siblings often sought her out as a substitute for their mother, who was almost always preoccupied with something else.

And, finally, Smita's 'period bug' arrived. Subha had, of course, neglected to speak to her about it but, fortunately, after all the educational discussions on the playground, Smita was prepared for it. She had only relatively minor cramps compared to some of the horrific tales told by her friends, and the amount of blood was completely manageable.

Smita was a little concerned, however, about the uncontrollable mood swings she had begun experiencing. She knew from her friends that this was hormonal, and part and parcel of getting her period; and she also knew that of course she was deeply saddened by the passing of Dadi, so that wouldn't have helped. But she recognised that there was an element of negativity to her emotions now, a feeling of being completely despondent and unhappy that had not existed in her world before, and these depressive states alternated with a raging anger, a feeling that she needed to rant and vent at someone otherwise she would explode.

ಹ 6 ಛ

1962: Cooking lessons

The leaves danced across the road, creating a carpet of mottled hues when settled on the newly tarred surface. Autumn was such a beautiful season. The rich reds and oranges were a stark contrast to the black road. If only she had a skirt that was so richly coloured.

Smita wished she could dance like the leaves and imagined herself in a long swishing skirt of beautiful ornate Indian fabric, swaying her hips in the way that the heroines in the Indian films did. She would rather be doing that than preparing herself for marriage, as her mother kept insinuating these days. She frequently thought her mother was a reincarnation of Mrs Bennett in Jane Austen's novel *Pride and Prejudice*.

Sometimes Smita wished that she lived in the Victorian era as depicted in those books, with its grand balls, the stunning dresses the women wore, the picturesque countryside and the picnics they all went on. On the other hand, it did seem a little boring, as the heroines didn't do much other than sit around and while away their time with frippery and folly.

Subha had hinted more than once that she wanted to find a suitable match for her girls – although her two elder daughters were only fourteen and ten, 'it was never too early', according to Ma. She also said that the suitors had to be from affluent families or have some source of acquiring wealth. These were, however, few and far between – as in *Pride and Prejudice*. And, also as in that story, Subha placed her own happiness above that of her daughters, thought Smita, crossly.

Subha herself would have preferred to have been married to someone from Durban, especially a man from one of the better-known business families that ran buses, fruit and vegetable market stalls, or takeaway establishments. She'd longed to live in a palatial home, with large numbers of rooms to accommodate all the sons she'd have, and their wives and families. And there obviously would have to be plenty of servants, as she would not be doing any housework.

Her father, however, had been very taken with the young Shankar: trained as a language and history teacher and almost finished his training as a Hindu priest, he would be ideal match for Subha, he thought, as she'd shown a strong inclination to being pious, observing all rituals and fasts with total faith and devotion, and learning the Hindi and Sanskrit Devanagari scripts most diligently. The old man felt a certain affection for his youngest daughter and, maybe because of her obvious intelligence, he often told her that she should have been born a boy so that she could take over his priestly duties from him. Of course, he had no idea how much that statement would affect her in later life, as she adored her father and thought that by being born female she'd disappointed him. She was thus determined to have sons so as not to disappoint her husband as well.

When she'd been introduced to Shankar, despite her disappointment that he was not a rich businessman from Durban, she had found him to be attractive, tall and broad shouldered, with a thin angular face, an aquiline nose and the lightest hazel eyes. He was unusually fair, a trait that was admired by most Indians, although it was more highly valued in a woman. Even though he was ten years older, he was an appealing prospect.

So, amid much pomp and ceremony, as was befitting of any Indian wedding, Subha was married at the family farm in Cato Ridge and afterwards moved with her new husband to the so-called City of Gold – which turned out to be a cold, dry, yellow-and-brown dump. This was especially the case on the East Rand, where Shankar and she had initially settled, in his parents' roomy but slightly run down home in the Germiston Asiatic Bazaar, straight after their marriage. Here, Subha had had to put up with living communally with her mother-in-law and Shankar's elder brother's wife, Devi, and a lack of proper plumbing that caused a nauseating stink to which she could never become accustomed. As Devi already had two sons, who she pampered continually, most of the housework and cooking became Subha's responsibility, but she did not mind too much as it kept her busy.

It took a while for Subha to discover that not all the Transvaal was as uniformly ugly as the suburb in which she lived. In central and northern Johannesburg, for example, there had been a concerted effort to plant many trees. These suburbs, whose names – Parkview, Parkwood, Craighall Park, Forest Town – evoked the green beauty of the surroundings, were reserved for whites. The only time an Indian family might find itself there would be on a weekend visit to Zoo Lake, a central feature in the area – one of the early mining magnates had gifted the land to the City of Johannesburg on condition it remained open to all races. The first time Subha and Shankar had gone to Zoo Lake on a Sunday had been wonderful, Subha remembered; the sun had shone brightly in a perfectly blue, cloudless sky over the shimmering lake bordered by many weeping willows and with colourful little boats scattered over its surface.

Shankar had decided early on that he would save enough money before he married so that his wife would have a comfortable life. Most of his peers were married in their early 20's but he had worked for his father as a taxi driver for a few years to earn money for his studies, and then had saved money after he had started his teaching job. After their marriage, as these savings accumulated, he and Subha had been able to relocate to Bakerton, the newer Springs counterpart of the Germiston Indian area. There, Shankar had built this sizeable family home on the small plot of land he'd bought, leaving little space for a garden or a vegetable patch. This did not make Subha happy, as she was used to the great expanse of outdoors on the farm, but a blessing was the mature peach tree in the small back yard, which yielded a great deal of fruit and kept her busy in summer making preserves and pickles. She often impressed her relatives in Natal with her peach jams from her own garden; mango and litchi trees might have been prevalent and treasured in Natal, but the Transvaal had its own special appeal.

Subha also planted some flowers and shrubs to add colour to the front garden, and herbs like coriander and mint, which she would use in her cooking, in a big old enamel bathtub in the back yard.

Subha was very skilled in the culinary arts. As a youngster growing up in Natal, she'd learnt to cook the food favoured by the Hindi-speaking people of South Africa, but now she also prided herself on her ability to replicate dishes with accuracy, and almost always with an improvement in the flavour of the original dish. She often discussed with her Gujarati neighbours their daily menus and didn't hesitate to adopt some of the exotic-sounding meals that these ladies prepared. Gujarati cooking seemed simpler in many ways than what she'd learnt at home from her mother.

ℵ ℭ

Smita was now old enough to start learning some basic cooking skills, Subha decided. The baby was due in a few months' time, and without Dadi to help, Subha would need Smita to step up. Martha was not allowed to help with the cooking – the family followed a strict vegetarian diet and as Martha did not, she could not be allowed close to the food preparation. Subha was also very particular about hygiene in the kitchen and she did not trust Martha with washing her hands properly after completing the housework, so she was not permitted to touch any of the food that was being cooked.

Indian cooking could be quite complex and there was so much to learn, so it was best that she start to teach her daughter now. The girl was too engrossed in her books anyway, Subha thought; who knew what strange ideas she might pick up from the novels she had her nose permanently stuck in? *Oliver Twist*, *David Copperfield*, *Silas Marner*, *Jude the Obscure* – why was Smita even reading about strange white boys? And *Jane Eyre* and *Emma* – white girls too, but all were foreign and the same to her. If Smita wanted to read so much, why couldn't she read the Hindu scriptures they owned?

It would do her daughter no good to be influenced by western ideas, and as her mother, Subha felt she needed to instil in Smita the values that an Indian wife should have. Shankar always indulged her, and he could not see how quickly she was growing up. After all, people had already enquired about her availability as a wife, since she was so tall for her age, and they thought that she was old enough to be married.

Subha heard Smita at the front door. 'Hello, Smeets. How was school today?' she called.

Smita was instantly suspicious, as her mother rarely referred to her by her childhood nickname – but then, she had to admit, she was feeling particularly moody today. Many of her friends were having these moods swings as well, and they often got into petty arguments and fights. Kala, her friend from across the road who had opinions about many matters as she had an elder sister, said that her sister said it was all part of growing up. But Smita definitely didn't want to end up as melancholy and unpredictable as her mother, who she tried to avoid spending time with her these days – she could get very impatient and sometimes unintentionally snap at her mother, and then was remorseful afterwards.

Subha, however, seemed to be on a mission. She took Smita's bag from her and gave her a brief hug, then shooed her in the direction of the bedrooms. 'Change out of your uniform and have some tea, then I'm going to start to teach you the first few things about cooking.'

'Oh no, Ma, not today. I have an important test tomorrow and I need to study,' said Smita in the most convincing voice that she could muster, hoping that this cookery lesson would be delayed. She really wanted to try and get full marks for the test, but she knew her mother did not really care about her academic performance. And she was longing to finish her new novel from the school library, *Wuthering Heights*. The story was utterly romantic and so sad. Would she ever have someone like Heathcliff to love her completely and eternally?

'Don't be silly, now,' Ma said. 'You think that a silly test is more important than real life lessons? When I was your age, I was made to leave school and I was helping to make the rotis every day, never mind how hot the weather was; you had to make the rotis fresh every night for supper, and to be near the stove in the heat. It was not easy. You girls have it much easier, especially now with the electric plates that we can use if the stove is not lit.'

Resigned to the cooking lesson, Smita went to her room to peel off her school uniform. She decided that she had to make the best of it and hoped that she would get to do some of the fun tasks, like mincing the ginger and garlic that was mandatory in almost every dish the family ate, or pounding spices – at least she would have a chance to vent her frustrations if she could hammer the pestle onto the special brass mortar that had come all the way from India, even though Subha constantly reminded her that she was 'banging down too hard'.

Smita could not understand the urgency to have all these lessons. As enjoyable and delicious that curries were, there were many other simple meals that one could survive on without complicated cooking – toasted cheese or peanut-butter sandwiches, potato chips in a sandwich, macaroni and cheese, or even plain buttered bread washed down with a glass of with Fanta or Sparletta.

The doorbell chimed and Smita heard Ma say, 'Oh, it must be the uncles from Fordsburg. Come, you can see what I buy from them and all the things that we need to use for cooking as well.'

The 'uncles' from Fordsburg were no one's uncles; they weren't even close to being related to them, as they were Muslim; it was just a term of respect. They had a grocery shop in Fordsburg, a suburb northwest of the city and one of the oldest areas of Johannesburg. They travelled to the many outlying areas that had Indian communities, including Middelburg, Springs and Germiston, to supply them with the spices needed for the preparation of curries, and they also had an assortment of lentils, pulses and dried beans.

Smita groaned as a show for her mother but in truth she actually loved it when the uncles visited, as the aromas of the fresh spices filled the air and it was quite fascinating to watch them with their little scale weighing out the dhals and filling the plastic bags. She wished that she could take those cylindrical metal weights and balance the weight of the spices by herself – it looked like a game that would entertain her for hours. She loved that removing or adding just a spoonful of any ingredient could make the scale tip to make both sides equal.

Subha bought whole coriander, cumin, fennel seeds, fenugreek seeds, mustard seeds, cloves, cardamom, aniseed and peppercorns, all in different quantities, as some of the spices were used more often than others. The cumin and coriander seeds had to be checked for stones and dirt, washed and left out to dry in the sun, after which they were powdered for use.

She also took some ground asafoetida, which helped to alleviate the gas emission of the beans and pulses.

Subha chatted to her daughter about her purchases as she prepared and packed them away. 'Some of the seeds are added whole to the oil first, to release their flavours. The cinnamon, cloves, cardamom and peppercorns are made into garam masalas, with coriander and cumin, which are lovely for flavouring meat and chicken. And the same powdered mixture can be used to spice up tea in winter – it has a delicious flavour that warms the body on the coldest days. And when these spices are added to ginger, they alleviate symptoms of the worst colds and sinusitis.'

Many of the seeds had medicinal value, Subha continued. 'You add thymol seeds to pastry dough to enhance the flavour and also to aid digestion once the dough has been fried,' she explained. Already in Subha's spice cupboard were cloves, which she gave to the girls when they had a toothache; turmeric, which she added to boiled milk and ginger for colds; and powdered nutmeg, which she mixed with honey when they had bad coughs.

In the kitchen, Smita learnt that there would be no pounding or hammering today, as the spices were ground already. 'First, let me show you how to chop onions,' Subha said.

This exercise caused Smita's eyes and nose to run, and she dragged her sleeved arm across her face.

Subha was horrified. 'Go and get a hanky, then wash your hands properly before you come back. Have I not told you that cooking is an absolutely clean job? At least your hair is neatly tied and not hanging about like some bhuthin!'

Subha had qualms about bodily fluids and food – in the ancient Vedic way, food had to be prepared with the greatest consideration for hygiene, so cooking should be done only after the morning ablutions were completed, and if you needed to go to the toilet again after you'd begun the food prep, you had to bathe again prior to resuming your duties at the stove – rules that Smita thought were extreme and ridiculous.

When Smita got back, her nose duly wiped and her hands washed, her next task to learn was cooking rotis. 'Wait for the little bubbles, then you can turn it over. For the second time that you turn it, there should be bigger bubbles. When you turn it over for the third time, the roti should swell like a balloon. If this does not happen, then you know you did something wrong ...'

Subha was taking her daughter's cooking education quite seriously, and she often dragged Smita into the kitchen when she got back from school to teach her yet another skill. The nuances of making dough were drummed into her. 'If the dough is not made properly, the roti turns out stiff and chewy like rubber or hard enough to break your teeth,' her mother warned her; to avoid this, the dough had to be made with boiling water and oil, and kneaded to perfection.

The rolling out of the roti was another skill that had to be mastered, and Smita's first attempts drew some uncomplimentary comments from her mother. Soon, though, Smita got the knack of it, producing pieces of dough that were moulded into circular discs to resemble perfect rounds. The thickness of the final product was just as important for the consistency and pliability of the cooked roti so that there were no dental catastrophes caused by the cook's inefficiencies.

Puri dough was next: it was made with warm water, sour milk and margarine or butter, not oil. Puris were rolled out thicker than rotis, and Ma prided herself on the fact that her puris always swelled to perfection when she fried them. 'The secret is that the frying oil must be exactly the right temperature, otherwise the puris are soggy and limp,' she told Smita.

Smita tried her best to please her mother, who was struggling under the weight of her fifth pregnancy. Smita was not sure how many pregnancies a woman was supposed to endure but five seemed a lot. Why anyone would want to subject themselves to this over and over again was a mystery to her.

This baby wasn't something that Smita was particularly looking forward to, as it would mean that she would need to come home from school earlier to help her mother with the newbie, and that would interfere with netball practice, and they had the interschool tournament coming up. Initially, when she'd brought home the consent form for her parents' permission to take part, Subha had been adamant that she would not be allowed to.

Smita had protested strongly. The tournament would be held at the school that Shankar taught at, so he would be present on the day and could easily keep an eye on her, she told her mother, and Subha finally – albeit reluctantly – agreed.

The issue with Smita representing her school at any sport these days were that some of the schools were 'mixed', and allowed coloured pupils to be admitted as well; there were no schools built specifically for either race group in the area. Since many of the coloured pupils were exceptionally skilled at netball and soccer compared to their Indian counterparts, they were frequently selected to represent their schools.

Smita wondered if they would ever play white or African schools, as it did seem odd that if this was a regional tournament, the only opponents that they had were other Indian schools. She knew that the pupils of other races played sport – she had noticed the massive sports fields at the white school in Springs town. It would have been a wonderful experience to play on those well-manicured fields. Some of her friends said that white schools had swimming pools as well, which seemed far-fetched to her.

Smita found it a bit strange to play against coloured pupils, as there were no coloureds at her school. She was intrigued by their varied appearances. Some were very dark-skinned, while others were as fair as white people, albeit with the kind of curly hair that made it obvious that they weren't white. Some of the girls were very pretty, with fair skin, light eyes and fleshy pink lips. Smita had heard that some coloureds could be 'reclassified' as white if they 'passed the pencil test', a process where a pencil was passed through the hair, and if the hair wasn't so kinky, the pencil came out the other end, but if the curls were too tight, then the pencil remained stuck in the hair and this meant the person had failed the test. It was really bizarre.

The perception of coloureds in the Indian community was generally negative, Smita conceded. After an altercation between some Indian and coloured boys a few years before at an interschool event, in which an Indian was the victim of a stabbing, Indian parents had become reluctant to send their children to these gatherings.

Smita enjoyed playing netball and was good at it. With her long legs, she could run competently, and her height was advantageous in assisting her to score goals for the team. She was regarded as one of the best players at her school, and there was a strong possibility of her being selected to play at regional level. Still, even if that did happen, Smita thought glumly, there was no chance of Subha permitting her to play at the Transvaal tournament.

Sometimes she wondered if these rules that her mother made really were for her own good, as Subha repeatedly insisted, since the main argument these days was against anything that would be of no benefit to her in her – Subha's – quest to find a suitable husband.

'You think any boy will be impressed by a girl who runs around like a horse chasing a ball? And so filthy and sweaty you get after being in the dust the whole day,' her mother said, tipping up her nose in disgust.

It didn't help that once Smita returned from a tournament with a swollen and bruised upper lip. She'd been accidentally hit in the face by a heavyset girl defending for the opposition. Subha had been beside herself, and furious with Shankar as well. 'See now how she looks! And you want her to go play this stupid netball-shwetball? What if she got more badly hurt? What would you do then? As it is, I have three daughters to find boys for, and so far, they all look pretty enough, but who will marry a disfigured girl?'

Despite the throbbing pain, Smita had grinned. Sure, her lip did look hideous, but she knew it would heal and the swelling would subside. And anyway, it had been worth it: despite the size and bullying tactics of the other team, Smita's team had managed to secure the winning spot.

The winter holidays were approaching but Smita had resigned herself to the fact that the family were probably not going to Durban this year, as she sensed her mother would not be able to make the trip.

On the day that they closed school for the holidays, Subha called her to her bedroom and opened the trunk she kept at the foot of her bed. 'There is this pretty emerald-green sari that I think you should try on, Smita, then I can sew the blouse for you. You know your cousin Rohini is getting married in two weeks' time, and I want you and Shruthi to go with Pitaji to the wedding. I can't make it, but since Rohini has no sisters, you two need to be there for her, to help with applying hurdee for the cleansing ceremony and eating the kheer with her in the morning.'

The eating of the kheer was the last meal the bride ate as an unmarried woman, and this was fed to her by her mother's brother, which was why Smita's father was to attend the wedding. He had one sister, Auntie Mala, and Shankar made it his duty to support her. He felt that his family had not been fair to her, as she was a female, so she had not inherited any of their late father's assets.

Mala had fallen in love with her husband when he had visited the family home with some of their relatives from Durban, where he was also from. Dadi had not been happy for her only daughter to be married so far away from the family but she was insistent that was what she wanted. Mala's life was also quite miserable as there were constantly rumours of her husband's Raj's infidelities – not that anyone would ever take these allegations seriously, as his family was well respected. Appallingly, many people even justified this abhorrent behaviour, cruelly noting that his wife was not an attractive enough match for him, so he was naturally inclined to stray from his marital bed.

Preparations for the trip were made, although without the normal excitement of a trip to Durban. Ma did not bake anything or make any special snacks for their trips, nor did they pack any new dresses. They would only be staying for a few days and not visiting all the relatives, as they usually did.

It was strange for Smita and Shruthi to be travelling with Pitaji alone, but fun as well. When Ma was there, she nagged him during the trip, and he tended to become grumpy. The girls were also exposed to Pitaji's more nurturing and caring side: he made sure that they had their tea and sandwiches, bought them sweet treats and chocolates when they stopped to refuel the car, and constantly asked if they needed to use the toilet. At home he never got involved in any of these mundane details of their lives.

The weather wasn't too pleasant, though. The day they left it was freezing, and they donned their hats and warm clothes, and took blankets to wrap around themselves while they sat in the car. Ma always packed blankets on their trips to Durban as the weather could be very unpredictable. Even in summer if there was inclement weather or fog in the mountainous areas of the Drakensberg or around the Natal midlands, there would be a chill in the air.

The passing scenery was drab, a dry and dusty monotony of yellowing grass overlaid with a layer of swirling dust. They passed nondescript towns on the way – Warden, Villiers, Harrismith – with clusters of houses and occasionally a steepled church or a school, and Smita wondered if anyone lived in these ghost towns, as they appeared completely uninhabited.

When they got off the highway for the routine bladder-emptying break, their breaths formed their own little clouds. If Pitaji wasn't within earshot, the girls would pretend that they were smoking, as they often did at school. It was too cold to picnic outside, so they sat in the car to eat and drink their tea, which as usual tasted of the plastic from the thermos – but it was comfortingly warm, and as it went down, it created a pleasant feeling that permeated their icy bodies and even seemed to reach down to their toes.

They reached Aunt Mala's house in Clare Estate, an Indian suburb of Durban, late in the evening, and instead of all the normal treats that they'd become accustomed to at their granny's house, at the farm in Cato Ridge, all they ate for supper at their aunt's was some watery lentils and rice. Even though their aunt denied that her family had financial difficulties, they always got the impression when they visited that either their uncle was extremely tight-fisted or there was a lack of money. Ma constantly sent their cousin, Rohini, hand-me-downs that the girls had outgrown, and she also passed on some of the offerings given to Shankar as part of the payment for his priestly duties – she did not always care for the quality of the rice or the towels or the shirts that were given to him.

Rohini was excited to see them but there was an air of sadness about her. She was young, only sixteen, and an eager pupil at school. However, when the marriage proposal was offered to her parents, they did not hesitate: girls were seen as a burden and it was best to get them married off as quickly as possible. It did not matter that she had to leave school; education was not considered a prerequisite for marriage.

Rohini looked fragile in her sari, with her skinny arms and washboard chest that Smita and Shruthi – both quite well endowed for their ages – giggled about. Smita looked like a full-grown young woman at fifteen and Shruthi at just eleven had already started showing signs of being curvaceous.

All three girls had fun that night, applying the turmeric paste and dancing to the imitations of popular Hindi film songs with some of the other ladies. The music was played outside in the little yard by some local musicians who were friends of their uncle. But when the party became a bit bawdy, and the men attending the function grew more and more lecherous proportional to the amount of liquor consumed, Pitaji sent his daughters into the house to go off to bed. These men who they were supposed to respect as elders were transformed in the dimly lit yard into leering, sniggering creatures that whispered disgusting comments to each other and winked suggestively at the girls. Some even had the audacity to pucker their lips into kissing signs at Smita when they thought no one was watching.

Smita was taken aback at their behaviour. Were all men this despicable? Then she thought about her father and some of her other uncles, who were quite different and would never purposefully embarrass any woman, and decided she was overreacting.

During the wedding the next day, despite there being no intoxicating substances available, there was still sufficient leering by the men to make her uncomfortable all over again. Rather than feeling pretty in the emerald sari, she felt exposed. The material was chiffon and sheer enough to show off some parts of her that were not normally on display, despite the extensive sequin work that created an opaque appearance.

It seemed to Smita that it wasn't only the men who were paying her unwelcome attention; some of the older women were also studying her and gossiping among themselves. And then there was a group of women around her mother's age who continually accosted her and her sister and insisted on kissing them. Smita hated the feel of their greasy lipstick on her skin, and the whiffs of halitosis she had to endure. She found this behaviour unfathomable: why would these female relatives, who barely knew her, openly display this sort of affection?

Later on, though, after the guests had left, when Auntie Mala was making up the extra beds for Smita and Shruthi in the area that served as a dining room and lounge, she dropped a clue. 'You know, Smita, you looked so pretty today, and a lot of the aunties with sons want you for their daughter-in-law,' she said, casually.

Smita felt as if a dagger had been plunged into her heart, causing excruciating pain. 'But I don't want to get married!' she wailed. 'I am still in school!'

This outburst was heard by everyone in the little house and Shankar emerged from the room he was sharing with some of his male relatives to find out what was going on. When Smita told him, he reassured her that she'd be allowed to finish school, and that he and her mother had no immediate plans to marry her off.

He explained that at weddings, young pretty girls were always stalked by the mothers of eligible young men, who wanted to make sure that they got the best of the bounty. Similarly, he said, some mothers shamelessly paraded their young daughters at these events to attract the attention of any interested parties. It made Smita thankful that her mother wasn't there – it seemed like the kind of thing she might do.

The next day, after a late breakfast, they left for home. The girls were soon asleep after the hectic weekend, and without Subha to distract him, Shankar was free to use the unusual quiet time to wonder about the ways of life.

Like Smita, he had noticed the women at the wedding gossiping about her and had overheard one or two mention how she would make a perfect match for a son or a brother's son or a husband's nephew. He was aware of how the matchmaking happened, and how necessary it was, but he felt uncomfortable that they were targeting his little girl so soon. He realised, of course, that his little brown-eyed girl was growing into a beautiful young woman but to think of her being married ... no. It was all happening too fast.

The problem was that Smita was tall and sometimes appeared older, but she was still way too young to be considering marriage, Shankar thought, crossly. Subha had been seventeen when he'd married her but even she had been allowed to get her junior certificate, the qualification awarded to a scholar who had completed the first phase of high school.

Well, life moved on, he mused, but as far as he was concerned, there were still a few years before he'd have to go through the ordeal of marrying off his eldest daughter. When it did happen, he knew that Subha would want the grandest ceremony they could afford, with all the bells and whistles, so it would take months of planning, shopping and possibly even renovations to the house. The mere thought of it wearied him.

꩜ ꩜

Smita's return to the third term of school was during an extremely cold and miserable spell. The icy weather was more difficult to endure as they had just returned from the mild and pleasant Durban winter. The wind was bitterly cold, nipping at any exposed area, with occasional icy rain shower. The boys were fortunate to be allowed to wear balaclavas, allowing them to cover their noses and mouths. But Smita's lips were exposed and constantly chapped, no matter how much Vaseline she applied, and her nose was forever cold.

Then one morning they awoke to a scene that made it all worthwhile: the ground was spread thinly with a layer of fluffy white snow. The fir trees on the open ground across the road from their house were sprinkled with white powder, painting a picture that was close to the European winter scenes depicted in books. Pitaji said that it had been at least twenty years since they'd last seen snow up here on the highveld.

All the children in the neighbourhood were absolutely thrilled and fascinated at this glorious spectacle and managed to scoop up sufficient amounts of the icy substance to make snowballs and even small snowmen. It was the stuff of fairy tales for them, and the beauty of the snowflakes floating down was a sight to behold.

Ma made special treats that afternoon: piping-hot cocoa with savoury eats, toasted cheese and roasted nuts, all so welcome after all the frolicking in the cold.

As the winter eased and the weather began to warm up, the family's evening visits to the temple became more frequent, as they did every year. As Pitaji was the priest in the area, he was the custodian of the temple, so the family accompanied him on the auspicious religious occasions during the year.

August heralded the start of many such occasions that were celebrated and observed. First was Raksha Bandhan, the day where brothers and sisters celebrated their love for each other; the sister tied a rakhee, or colourful string, around her brother's wrist to show her love for him, while the brother promised to protect his sister from harm for the rest of their days. Girls without a brother could tie the rakhee for close male friends or other close male relatives. Ma was always commenting on how sad it was that the girls did not have their own brother to cement this bond with.

Raksha Bandhan coincided with Lakshmi Puja, the day on which a prayer dedicated to the goddess Lakshmi is performed, to ask for her blessings for prosperity in all aspects of life. On this day, celebrants came to school with a bright red string around their wrists.

But the biggest religious occasion for Smita's family was Krishna Janamasthami, the commemoration of the birth of Lord Krishna, the avatar of Lord Vishnu who'd appeared on earth to save it from destruction by demons. The family observed eight days of fasting until sunset, singing hymns at the temple, meditation on the deity, making a variety of sweet offerings daily, and adorning the idols and pictures of Krishna and Vishnu with fresh flowers, and draping them with different-coloured pieces of cloth. The sweets to offer to the gods prepared by the women who attended the evening prayer at the temple were always so delicious, especially after fasting for the entire day. The sweets ranged from fresh coconut in sugar with raisins and almonds to delicacies made with semolina or chickpea flour.

Smita loved these times at the temple, and not only because they were a welcome break from the normal routine. Now, as she was fifteen, she got to wear Ma's colourful cast-off saris and shawls. Singing the melodious devotional songs in unison created a harmony so uplifting that the atmosphere was quite ethereal, especially with the wonderful aromatic scent of the incense sticks and the arrays of pretty flowers and fabrics on the altar. She knew she had a good singing voice, as people always encouraged her to lead the bhajans and kirtans. And because she was part of the family of the priest, not only did she help to prepare beforehand and clean up afterwards, but, as Ma was indisposed due to her ever-increasing size, she got to distribute the flowers and other offerings that the people brought to the temple for the congregation, as the blessings were shared by all those who attended.

The culmination of the celebrations was the day thought to be Krishna's actual appearance or birth on earth. On this day, they had a tiny figurine in the form of the baby Krishna, which they placed in an ancient wooden cradle near the altar, and which, at midnight, the devotees rocked while chanting 'Glory to Lord Krishna' in Sanskrit and placing flowers on the baby.

Smita sometimes mused about the similarity of this to the nativity scene that was enacted in the school play at the end of every year about the birth of baby Jesus but she kept these thoughts to herself as she suspected they may have been almost blasphemous.

The temple had been built after most of the houses in the Bakerton had already been erected, so it was on the periphery of the area, which meant that the walk home took them through the newer, poorer section. While walking home after some of these celebrations one evening, with Pitaji and some of the other male devotees a few steps ahead of them, she and Shruthi took the opportunity to steal a glance at Kanamma's house, as they remembered the wonderful little deities and shrine they had seen there when Ma had visited. Through the uncurtained windows they could see that whole room was bathed in the light of many lamps, and that Kanamma had also decorated the statues with shimmering pieces of cloth and garlanded them; the aroma of incense wafted through the air.

Looking ahead to make sure that Pitaji was deep in conversation with the other men, Smita quickly entered the little house and bowed down at the shrine, taking the blessings from the volatile smoke of the camphor that was burning. Kanamma, who was seated at a small table nearby, looked up in surprise, but then simply gave Smita a beautiful smile that radiated calmness. It may have been rumoured that she was a witch, but Smita knew that this could not be true, as she had such a serene and kindly demeanour.

The atmosphere here was so peaceful and welcoming that she wanted to stay but Shruthi was pulling at her and motioning her out of the door before anyone saw them.

Smita reluctantly followed Shruthi down the road, catching up with their father, but she wished she could spend more time with that amazing woman, and was disappointed with the community for not recognising Kanamma's obvious power that came from her steadfast faith and devotion.

1962: A son at last

Spring arrived with its promise of new life, pretty buds emerging from flowering plants and leaves unfurling on the trees. Then there was the arrival of the first rains, which caused a sporadic return of some cold weather but the delicious scent of the rain after the dry winter months more than compensated for the slight discomfort.

It was on one of these rainy days, while they were huddled in the kitchen over popcorn and cocoa, that Ma experienced her first labour pains. She cooked supper but afterwards said she needed to lie down, and a few hours later Pitaji informed them that her waters had broken, and he took her to the hospital.

Although Meera's delivery had gone quickly and easily, Subha wasn't getting any younger, and didn't want to take any chances, and she and Shankar had decided long in advance that this would be a hospital birth.

The girls waited apprehensively for Pitaji's return but, sleepy after an uneventful supper, they huddled together on one bed and slowly nodded off. It was the first night Meera had ever spent away from her Mama, and this made her fretful, but with a bit of extra attention from Smita, she was mollified.

Smita heard Pitaji arrive home some time during the early hours of the morning but was too tired to rouse herself from the sandman's comfortable embrace.

The next day the girls were up bright and early, and immediately went to ask Pitaji about the new baby. Beaming with pride, he told them that their prayers had been answered: they finally had a baby brother! He said that the birth had been fairly straightforward, and that he would fetch Ma and the new baby that afternoon, so Smita helped Martha make up her parents' bed with fresh linen and ensured that the younger girls made a special effort to look pretty. After this she prepared a rich, hearty meal supplemented by breads and snacks given to them by the neighbours. Grudgingly, she admitted that Ma's cooking lessons had paid off. She smiled to herself, acknowledging, too, that Ma had planned in advance for these days.

Subha arrived home with a radiant smile and a little package tightly swaddled. According to the Panchang, a compilation of astrological predictions for the year that Pitaji had posted to him from India every year, the baby had been born during an unlucky time. But if a few vital rituals were performed to placate the spirits and appease the gods, the bad luck would be warded off. Even this, which normally would have worried Subha, did not seem to affect her joy at the arrival of a son.

The girls were summoned to say hello to their new bhai. 'You girls are so lucky now – you have your own brother to tie a rakhee for, instead of your friends' brothers and the neighbours!' Ma crowed.

For Smita to see her mother looking so happy was a blessing in itself; she couldn't recall when last she'd seen Ma so satisfied with herself. It was a huge change from when Meera was born, but Smita tried her utmost to brush away these uncharitable thoughts. Fortunately, neither of the other girls was old enough to realise the difference in their mother's reaction to this birth but it was something that Smita could not come to terms with or forgive.

For the next few weeks, Subha was wholly preoccupied with her new acquisition. The family performed a thanksgiving yajna for the birth of the baby, in addition to the normal six-day naming ceremony. The baby was named Gautam, 'remover of darkness'. Subha thought that it was particularly apt, as this son would take away the darkness that had pervaded her life for the past few years.

This time, Smita's parents invited more guests than they had for previous new babies, to show off their heir.

Smita really thought that this talk of an 'heir' was a little ridiculous – her family was not royalty for her mother to have to produce a male heir! Even with British royalty, females could inherit the crown, so this term really irked her. Maybe it would have been more relevant or made more sense in a family that had a business or a farm to run, but what exactly would this little son inherit?

Subha hinted to some of the neighbours that they would have a priest in the making for the next generation.

৪৩ ৫৪

It was a happy and busy time for Shankar, too. He had many responsibilities to the community, as it was the time of the year when many people observed Pitrpaksh, a series of rituals carried out to ensure that the souls of departed family members were appeased. The traditional accompaniment to the prayer that was performed was the offering of food: a few of the deceased's favourite dishes were prepared, and a serving was placed in the garden, for consumption by birds, which were sometimes thought to represent the spirits of people who'd passed on. Certain households also put out alcohol or cigarettes if these had been enjoyed while the person lived.

In previous years, Subha had become melancholy around this time, as she remembered her twin baby sons, but this year she was too preoccupied with her living son to dwell on the past. And, in contrast with her slow recovery times after the birth of the twins and then Meera, this time she was up and bustling around the house within a week.

Still, Smita was kept busy. Although Subha took on the lioness's share of the baby-related work, such as feeding and changing, and bathing and putting to bed, Smita would take over these tasks when her mother had to have a bath or needed to cook. Sometimes, Subha would be so exhausted from a series of nights of interrupted sleep that she had to have an afternoon nap, and then Smita was the only daughter old enough to see to her little brother.

Smita was also in charge of entertaining the incessant stream of visitors who always seemed to arrive at the most inopportune moments, like when her little brother needed a nappy change or to be fed, or when Subha needed to drain her engorged breasts – although Gautam was suckling regularly, Subha was producing so much milk that the baby couldn't consume it all.

All of these bodily functions that had to be tended to, for both mother and baby, were unpleasant, thought Smita, especially when she was changing a nappy and the baby decided to shoot up an arc of urine that hit her in the face. She scrubbed many times but she felt that the odour seemed to linger. If one of her friends had to visit now, she would be mortified. The other disgusting thing was when the baby had to be burped after a feed and would bring up some milk which inevitably landed on Smita's clothes and left her reeking of vomit.

It was intriguing to her that her mother had done all of this for all her children and had not tired of the process. She had heard somewhere that a mother's love was like rays of sunshine – enough to spread around to all her children. Was it really like that? Perhaps, if it was your own baby, you became immune to the smells and grossness of it all.

One thing that Smita could not deal with, though, were the bodily changes and indignities that a woman had to go through to have a baby. She'd watched her mother swell up with her pregnancies to the point where it seemed like she would explode, and then her breasts also became huge and were often painful. The birth itself was such a scary process. Smita wondered how an entire baby could fit through a woman's vagina. Surely the pain was unbearable? She remembered her mother's screams from long ago. She also knew from the previous pregnancies that there was always a lot of blood. Then, after the birth, there was the eternal breastfeeding, as if the new mom were a human cow! And if she didn't get rid of the milk quickly enough, her breasts got hard and painful, and she had to insert smelly cabbage leaves into her bra for relief.

And Smita didn't even want to consider the other parts of the body that were affected. At one time she had gone into her mother's room without knocking and had seen Subha astride the embers of the fire that had been lit for the baby. Frankincense and thymol seeds had been added to the fire to create fumes that were aromatic and soothing. For the baby it had a dramatic and wonderful effect, as he slept soundly, while for the mother, the fumes, enhanced by the addition of garlic peels to create more smoke, assisted in the healing process if she had stitches 'down there'. Apparently, the addition of syringa leaves to the new mother's bath water had the same healing effect.

It was at this time that Smita particularly missed her granny, as there was often no adult available to scold her sisters when they got into irrational squabbles over who got the chair next to the fire in the kitchen, whose turn it was to pack away the dishes, whose socks were in whose drawer or who had stolen the only sharpened pencil in the house. Sometimes, she longed to be part of these fights, as she felt she had too much responsibility. She resented the fact that her sisters were allowed to attend the little community school that taught Gujarati every afternoon, which meant an extension of their playtime with their friends, while she had to be at home to take care of some or other chore. Most of her close friends were at Gujarati lessons too, and she would have loved to be there. And she knew that with her flair for languages, she would have excelled.

However, as Gautam grew older and more and more adorable,

matters started improving. Also, as the baby became less demanding, Ma grew more pleasant too, and started taking over her normal routine responsibilities.

In fact, Subha had recovered so well that she decided to perform a prayer that involved the raising of a red flag to show her appreciation to Hanuman, the monkey god, who symbolised strength and power, and would thus bestow these positive blessings on her little boy. In the war with the demon Ravana, the story went, Hanuman flew a red flag indicating victory; the modern-day symbolism of the flag for a Hindu was to garner Hanuman's support and strength to overcome all obstacles in life. The flag was triangular in shape, to resemble the pennants that were flown during times of war.

Subha became completely engrossed in the preparations for the event, sewing a flag into a triangle, with loops for the flagpole, edged with a white border and appliquéd with the 'Om' symbol. She positioned the flag in a corner of the front garden, facing east.

Ecstatic about the 'completion' of her family with the arrival of the male baby, Subha then informed Pitaji that they needed an updated family photograph; the last one had been taken on Smita's second birthday and showed only Smita as a toddler with her parents; neither of her sisters had, apparently, been considered crucial enough for a new family portrait.

Smita was excited at the prospect of a studio photograph, and the night before, the older girls put their hair in pin curls. Smita and Shruthi helped each other with the process of curling the hair and securing it with clips so that they would have beautiful, bouncy curls in the morning. Smita attempted to do the same with Meera but was not successful as she refused to sit still for long enough, and complained that the clips were hurting her.

They all donned their newest dresses, with Ma in an elegant sari and Pitaji in a suit. The photographer was a kind old gentleman who made them all strike serious expressions, portraying a prosperous and perfect family.

Having her mother back on household duties freed up Smita to indulge in her books, and to listen to the radio and the weekly hit parade that she documented carefully to observe the movement of the popular English songs up and down the charts. She'd then compare notes with her friends so they could make their own predictions about the new number one.

Most mothers didn't approve of their daughter's obsession with western pop music and encouraged their children to listen to their vernacular songs if they owned gramophones. When people visited India, they would sometimes bring home Indian music records.

Smita was fortunate that her family had always owned a gramophone and they had more recently acquired a record player, so she was never deprived of music. It was just lucky that Shankar loved music, and that records were one of his few indulgences that he encouraged in his children. His collection comprised music from Bollywood films, some religious music and recordings of Indian classical music.

Interestingly, it was Subha who'd insisted that the family have a radio at home; she'd told her husband that it was so lonely when he was away so often, that she needed some entertainment. So Smita also got to listen to the daily news bulletins, the weather forecast and sometimes some hilarious comedy skits.

Subha thoroughly enjoyed the soap operas on the radio, which often had sagas of illicit relationships, doomed love stories and general family drama. These stories struck a chord with most housewives, whose emotions were often suppressed.

1964: An unexpected addition to the neighbourhood

The stillness of the night was occasionally punctuated by the sound of the goods train that transported the coal from the Springs diggings to the gold mines on the Witwatersrand. The railway track was about a mile from the house but was still very audible.

Sometimes there was also a disturbance caused by the blasting from the coal mines, which caused the windows to shudder. The blasting was often done at night to reduce the exposure of the workers to the resulting smoke, dust and fumes, and – doubtless more importantly – so as not to affect productivity during daytime work hours.

Residents had long adapted to these percussive night-time intrusions and mainly everyone slept through peacefully. However, when a blood-curdling yell pierced the wee hours one night, everyone in the close vicinity woke up in terror.

Smita, who hadn't been asleep – she was up, studying – quickly ran through to her parents' bedroom, where her father was already swinging his legs out of bed, his hair standing on end. By the time Pitaji had walked through to the front room, switched on the light and peered through the venetian blinds, the yelling had died down to a keening sound, but it was still very loud. Many of the surrounding houses also had their lights on.

It was obvious to Shankar that the sounds were emanating from the house directly opposite theirs, so he donned a hat and dressing gown to protect him from the winter chill as he ventured out. As the priest, if someone had passed on, it was appropriate that he was there to offer solace and sympathy to the bereaved. Although, he thought, as he crossed the road, he could not imagine who would have passed on in that house, as the couple who lived there, and young adult son, Mahesh, had been hearty and healthy the last time he'd seen them.

Smita, peeping through the blinds, could see, in the unforgiving light of the neighbour's porch lamp, some people huddled around something on the ground, and the lady of the house clutching something to her chest. Unable to contain her curiosity any longer, Smita snuck out the front door and crept across the tiny front garden. Hiding behind the low garden wall, she managed to get a one-eyed view through the gate.

There seemed to be an argument developing. 'He can't be moved,' someone said. 'We must call the ambulance.'

Just then the group of people parted, and Smita's breath caught in her throat. Mahesh was lying unconscious on the porch, eyes swollen shut, hair and clothes soaked with blood. One of his arms lay limp and at a curious angle by his side – it was clear it was broken.

From the movement and crying that was emanating from the bundle his mother was holding, it was obvious it was a baby, but Smita could not fathom where it would have come from, as there were no young women in the house.

Now Mahesh's father was explaining in a loud voice to Pitaji what had happened. 'A vehicle arrived. Someone persistently knocked on the front door. When I opened it, there were two white men, who thrust this baby' – here the man gestured at the wriggling bundle – 'into my arms.'

Next, the man pointed to his son, lying still on the ground. 'They told me they could have done worse to him but the "stupid whore" who'd been entertaining him wouldn't stop screaming. They told me to tell my "filthy son" to keep his pants on and to leave white women alone. They told me not to call the police, as then Mahesh would be charged with being in contravention of the Immorality Act.'

The man pointed back at the crying baby, being held by the woman who was now also crying loudly. 'They told me they were "good Catholics" so they couldn't kill the "tiny bastard", and that my wife and I would have to raise the "half breed".'

Smita, horrified, ran back inside, just as Subha was coming out of her bedroom, clutching Gautam to her chest. 'What's happening?' she asked.

'They beat up Mahesh!' Smita shouted. 'He has a baby! No-one wants to look after the baby!'

Subha, too stunned to reprimand her eldest daughter for running outside in the middle of the night and minding everyone else's business, immediately pushed Gautam into Smita's arms and rushed out to see if she could help. Within a few minutes she was back, the bawling bundle held tightly in her arms.

'Boil some water, Smita, quick. This baby needs feeding,' she said, digging around in the kitchen cupboards for the tin of infant feeding formula she knew she had squirrelled away there.

Gautam had miraculously fallen asleep amidst all the commotion, so Smita was able to put him back in his cot in her parents' room. And, while the neighbours and Pitaji waited on their front stoep for the arrival of the ambulance, whose siren wails they could eventually hear coming closer, Smita and Subha fed the neighbour's baby, and bathed him, and dressed him in some of Gautam's baby clothes, which Subha had not yet found the heart to throw out or pass on. Smita was fascinated with how pale the little boy was, with skin so translucent that the blue veins could be seen through it. His skin reminded her of Pitaji's, especially on his legs and feet when he put on shorts and sandals during the summer months after being covered up and out of the sun all winter.

Once the ambulance had fetched the patient and was noisily making its way back to the hospital, Pitaji returned. Ma quickly put together a package containing more baby clothes and the rest of the tin of powdered infant formula, and sent Pitaji back over the road with the baby and these gifts.

ℰ ℭ

The baby, who was named Nirved, meaning 'gift', ended up transforming the lives of his grandparents, who adored him with all their hearts. Mahesh was their only son, so they considered the unexpected arrival of the baby, despite the circumstances of horror and embarrassment, to be a blessing.

Nirved was brought up in the traditional Hindu way and was taught Gujarati, so there would be no probing questions asked about his appearance: his jet-black hair contrasted shockingly with his extremely fair skin, grey-green eyes and raspberry-hued lips. In colouring, Smita observed again, he very closely resembled her own father, whose hair, although now shot through with grey, was also dark, but whose complexion and eyes were similarly pale.

Subha also had a soft spot for the little boy, which was just as well, as he was constantly in and out of their home, having no children of his own age to play with nearby. However, he also loved being around Subha, as she indulged him, and they did seem to have a special bond.

As for poor Mahesh, he returned from the hospital with some unfortunate scars on his face, paralysis in his arm – the nerve damage had been too great to be repaired – and a limp that would last his lifetime.

More importantly, though, while he recovered, his father had met with a Home Affairs official – they were all white – and handed over an envelope stuffed with banknotes, to make sure that the baby's race was registered as Indian. The money also ensured that the mother's personal details, especially her race, were overlooked. That way, Mahesh wouldn't face jail time for having had sexual intercourse with a white person – something that was prohibited by law by the South African apartheid government.

〄 9 ॐ

1964: Another departure; another arrival

The air was filled with the acrid smell of smoke issuing from the chimneys of the fortunate people who had coal stoves in their homes, and from the caretakers from the school nearby who burnt fires outside in huge steel drums called bowlas. The smell was comforting, somehow, despite the burning sensation in her nostrils, and it provided a distraction from inhaling the icy air.

Smita wistfully examined her chapped and scuffed hands as she chopped some of the firewood into kindling to start the morning fire in the coal stove in the kitchen. Wood was always used to start the fire, then the coal was added to prolong the life as well as increase the intensity of the fire, as the dirty black fuel burnt at a much higher temperature than wood. It was freezing cold again this morning, and the little back yard was rimmed with frost. Chopping firewood and hauling it inside to start the kitchen stove wasn't her usual morning chore – it was normally Martha's job. But Martha had been arrested the previous night.

There had been a deafening, pounding noise at about half past nine, when they were all preparing for bed. In the kitchen, Pitaji had just filled the last hotwater bottle that they all used to warm their frozen toes, and was locking up, when it seemed as if someone was breaking down the wooden gate in the back yard that opened onto the lane.

A voice shouted, 'Is iemand daar? Maak oop gougou of ons sal die hek breek!'

Pitaji shooed away the girls, who were all staring open-mouthed out of the kitchen window, trying to discern who was creating the racket outside. 'Go away, girls,' he whispered. 'I need to see what these men need.' Pushing them gently out of the kitchen and down the hall towards the bedrooms, he continued in a soft voice filled with fear and concern, 'Look in on Ma and tell her not to panic. Just tell her that I said that it must be some routine check.'

Leaving the girls in the passageway, Pitaji went back into the kitchen and Smita heard him shout, 'Ek kom, meneer. Wag 'n bietjie, asseblief.'

As soon as Pitaji went out the back door, Smita ran back into the kitchen so she could see what was happening outside. She watched her father struggle to unlock the padlock, and was shocked to see that as soon as it snapped open, the people on the other side shoved the gate ajar, forcing Pitaji back and to one side.

'Waar is die Basutho?' shouted a voice.

'Ekskuus, meneer?'

'Die Basutho meisie wat hier werk, jou stupid coolie.' The voice belonged to the man in front, who was in full South African Police uniform, wearing a cap with a big badge on it. Behind him were two more shadowy figures.

Smita watched her father stand up straight and his back stiffen at the insult. 'I am not aware of what you are talking about,' he said, slowly and clearly.

'Waar is haar kamer, her room? We know you coolies keep them holed up somewhere. And we need her papers.' The policeman, who Smita could see by the light cast out the kitchen door, was fat. And apparently angry about something.

Pitaji's shoulders slumped – it was clear he knew he was beaten.

On slow feet, he led them to the room with the outside door, and knocked on it. 'Martha, I'm sorry to disturb you, but there are some ... gentlemen here to see you,' he called.

The door opened immediately – evidently, Martha had heard everything and knew there was no escape. The fat bossy policeman pulled Martha out by her arm; Smita heard her gasp in shock and pain.

'Sit there and don't move,' he growled, pushing Martha down onto her haunches. Then he indicated to his two henchmen that they should go into Martha's room. 'Look for her papers,' he instructed.

Smita sat, frozen, crouched at the back kitchen door, listening to the sound of Martha's room being torn apart. Occasionally something came flying out the door to her room – once, a chair, which hit the ground with such force that one leg broke off; then a small pile of magazines, which scattered across the cement.

'Geen dokumente, Luitenant,' one of them finally reported.

The fat policeman turned on Martha. 'Waar's jou pasboek, meisie?' he shouted.

Martha began to cry, big, heaving sobs.

The policeman sneered. 'Don't turn on the waterworks, hey,' he said to her, then turned to Pitaji. 'The scum,' he said, 'they come here and corrupt the mine workers, prostituting themselves for next to nothing, and, you know, where there are women involved, they also make trouble.'

'Martha is a domestic worker. She is not a prostitute,' Pitaji said, but Smita could hear his voice wavering, as if he wasn't sure. Or maybe he was just scared. Smita herself was terrified.

'Get up,' the policeman instructed Martha, nodding at his henchmen to help her. Each took an arm and hauled her to her feet. 'You're going back to Basutoland, where you belong,' one of them told her.

'I have permission to work here!' Martha wailed. 'I have a work permit! I got it from the Bantu Authority!'

101

'You can tell the judge that,' the fat policeman said. 'Put her in the wagon,' he told the other two, who pulled Martha across the yard and towards the back gate.

Martha, suddenly realising that they were taking her to jail, and having heard terrible stories of what happened to Africans in white South African prisons, began struggling for her life. As Smita watched, horrified, one of the men quickly took a baton from a loop on his belt and struck out at Martha with it, once, twice, three times. Smita heard the sickening sound as it connected with bone.

Martha dropped to the ground, and the two men, each holding onto an arm, dragged her out the gate.

For the next few hours, the shaken family tried to make sense of the horrific intrusion into their peaceful life. Having made sure that Subha was okay – she was expecting again, and in no condition to weather this kind of shock – and that the two younger children were asleep, Pitaji took Shruthi and Smita into the kitchen with him, and sat down with them at the big table.

'You girls are old enough now to know what's going on in this country,' he began, looking seriously at both of them. 'There's a thing called apartheid, which means that people with light skins and people with darker skins aren't allowed to be friends. And all the best things are kept for the people with light skins. There isn't any rational reason for this – we with our darker skins are just as good in every way as the people with light skins. It's just some wicked white people in the government who have decided this.'

Smita stared at her father with his light skin and pale eyes. Even though she was almost an adult herself, there was still so much about the adult world that she didn't understand.

'And people with dark skins – black people, Africans – who live in neighbouring countries aren't allowed to be in South Africa without the proper paperwork,' Pitaji continued. 'The police are constantly looking for excuses to harass people and exert their power over the Africans, so they have routine raids to send these immigrants back to their countries. The problem is that these people from the neighbouring countries need money desperately, as sometimes their men leave to work on the mines in South Africa, and do not return home, often leaving no source of income to support the family. This is what happened with Martha: she has her own children, her parents, and other members of her extended family to support.'

'So does Martha not have a husband?' Shruthi asked.

'She does but she doesn't know where he is,' Pitaji said. 'He came to work on the mines. She heard that he had been working on the East Rand, but that he had died in a mine accident. It was while she was trying to find out all this that she ran out of money and had to find a job, and that's how she ended up working for us.'

'But why doesn't she have the right papers?' Smita asked.

Pitaji just shook his head. Smita didn't know if that mean that he didn't know, or if he just didn't want to go into it.

Later, lying in bed and unable to sleep because of everything that had happened that night, Smita fondly remembered some of the conversations that she had had with Martha on the way to the Chinaman's shop to pick up odds and ends for Ma. Ma always sent her along with Martha, as she did not trust Martha with the money.

Compared to when she was busy cleaning the house, Martha was a different person on their little walks to the shops, and sometimes she would skilfully bounce and hop over a tennis ball or show Smita her agility with a skipping rope. They also once or twice spent a little of the change from the shopping on the slap chips that were sold in the fruit and vegetable shop run for the workers by the Patels. Smita knew she would be in dire straits if her mother ever discovered that she had done this, but the whiff of the fried chips coupled with the mouthwatering aroma of the vinegar made her salivate, and she had convinced Martha to get some. As good a cook as her mother was, and as much as she loved curries, the taste of these chips was heaven – from the soft soggy texture to the way the vinegar assaulted her tastebuds and stimulated her salivary glands to go into overdrive, the experience was like no other.

'You know, Smeets, I miss my home,' Martha once told her. 'There in Basutoland, it is better. So much space, no smoke to make you cough, no ugly smells of the mine. And it is so quiet.'

'Smeets, what are you doing?' came Shruthi's voice from inside the house. 'Ma wants the fire, and we're all waiting to wash and have tea!'

Ma, suffering through her sixth pregnancy, was experiencing some back pain, but she knew it was not severe enough to be in labour. She was in a foul mood because of this and was incessantly cursing Pitaji for not being at home when she needed him the most.

Earlier that morning, while they were still in bed, the girls had overheard a tiff between their parents through the bedroom wall, with Ma trying to convince Pitaji to stay at home in case she needed him to drive her to the hospital, and he being adamant that he had to perform the wedding ceremony for the Mohan family, as they knew no other priest and had sent out many invitations with guests from Durban, so how could he let them down? Subha had accused her husband of putting other people before his own family. 'How can you abandon me at a time like this?' she'd wailed, as he'd walked out the door.

Smita and Shruthi gossiped about this, as they knew that most of the money that Pitaji made was given to Ma, and then there was the seedha, supposedly a token offering of food in return for the Brahmin or priest performing a prayer; in reality, Pitaji's congregation often gifted him a substantial number of groceries.

As it happened, by the time Pitaji arrived home late in the afternoon, the baby had still not arrived. 'See? You were just being dramatic this morning,' he told his wife. 'I knew your pains were not really that bad or so frequent that you could have been in labour. I would not have gone if I'd thought that you were really going to have the baby.'

Subha, who was still experiencing sporadic back pain, stared furiously at her husband. She was in no mood to be told that she was wrong.

Not wishing to further upset his extremely pregnant and volatile wife, Pitaji made her some tea and gave her a hot-water bottle to hold against her back, and encouraged her to breathe, and to walk around and squat to alleviate the pain.

When Subha finally fell asleep, Pitaji helped the girls prepare a sumptuous meal of a hearty bean stew accompanied by rotis, after which they enjoyed succulent oranges for dessert. The orange peels were then roasted on the coal stove, which imparted a wonderful citrus aroma in the kitchen.

Smita marvelled at how her father seemed able to always remain calm and keep them happy under the most trying circumstances. However, she knew that sometimes he used prayer as a form of therapy and escapism so he could maintain his sanity.

The peace in the home was short-lived, however, as within an hour Ma's waters had broken, and Pitaji had bundled her into the car. Smita was once again left in charge of her siblings, with the neighbours also alerted to keep an ear and eye open and lend a hand if necessary. The girls sang to Gautam and told him stories, cuddling together in their parents' bed until they all fell asleep.

Early the next morning, Manav, the neighbour's son, woke them by rapping on the bedroom window. He'd been knocking at the front door for about ten minutes, he told them. He'd been sent by his mother to help the girls with chopping kindling for the stove, as she'd heard through the domestic workers' grapevine that Martha had been taken away.

Manav had developed a recent infatuation for Smita, who'd initially found it rather flattering but now considered it simply an annoyance. He was only fourteen and she was seventeen now. Often, he would wait for her in the mornings to walk her to school, which was so embarrassing. He'd even taken to waiting for her in the afternoons to walk her home. She sometimes tried to walk fast to get away from him, but he was persistent and it didn't always work.

Manav's mother had also sent some fresh hot spicy griddle pancakes made with fenugreek leaves for their breakfast. Smita loved them and was grateful to his mother despite her irritation with Manav. And, truth be told, she was also grateful that he'd produced the kindling for the stove and helped her haul in sufficient coal to keep the fire burning for many hours.

Realising that she could do with his help getting all the children ready for the day too, she invited him to join them for breakfast. Shruthi was spoilt and moody and would only help Smita if she was forced to. Surprisingly, Ma did not admonish her for this behaviour. Smita wondered about this and thought that it might be because of the resemblance between the two of them.

After the meal, Manav and Shruthi got busy playing cards while Smita prepared the rice and lentils for lunch.

Manav had left by the time Pitaji returned about mid-morning, looking exhausted. It was strange to see him with day-old stubble as he was usually always bathed and shaved before the girls awoke. Only after these ablutions, obeisance to the sun god Surya and his daily morning prayers would he have something to eat.

'Is Ma okay? Is the baby fine? Is it a boy or a girl? When are they coming home?' Smita and Shruthi fired questions at their father.

He smiled at them but there was sadness in his eyes. 'This is a special day, my dears. You have been blessed with another little brother.' Then, looking grim, he indicated that they should come and sit down in the kitchen with him, so he could discuss something with them. Once they were seated at the table, a daughter on either side of him, he said, 'The baby had a small birth defect. He has only one functional hand. His other hand looks a bit like a lobster claw. Don't be afraid when you see him. The doctors call it ectrodactyly. It's very rare –it happens in only one in ninety thousand births.'

'What's a lobster?' Shruthi asked.

'It's a sea creature, with claws a little like a crab's,' Pitaji said.

The girls stared at him with big eyes.

'But your brother's hand isn't hard like a claw; it's tiny and soft, don't worry, and he is such a sweet-looking baby.'

Subha and the baby, Ramu, came home the next day. The delivery had been difficult, and Subha had many stitches 'down there'. The neighbourhood ladies dispatched the midwife Hansaben to assist with the healing, and the bathing and massaging of the new baby and the mother, as was common practice.

There was also another maid sent to help with the housework. They all appreciated the help but she was taciturn woman who did not want to engage in conversation very much with them. Smita did not blame her, as she had thought a lot about the hardship endured by the African domestic workers after Martha had been taken away. Pitaji had enquired at the police station a few times but the police pretended that they had no knowledge of any arrests of innocent women.

They never heard anything further about Martha and Smita often wondered what had happened to her, hoping that she managed to get home safely to be with her children.

The house was a hub of activity for the next few days. There was the normal three-day herbal bath, the daily ritual of massages with various warmed oils, the usual burning of the special fire which effused the wonderful aroma of the frankincense that was sprinkled over it. Ma's tummy was compressed and tied down with a wad of calico to help it shrink and return to its original shape. The sixth-day prayer to the ancestors to bless the baby was also done.

A thanksgiving prayer was offered once the twelve-day 'unclean' period that followed all childbirth events was over, with a hawan to cleanse the house and ask for a blessing to ward off the ill fortune that seemed to have been bestowed on this poor little mite. This was only done as Ramu was born at a time when the planets were not properly aligned, which meant that the baby would experience bad luck if the prayer was not performed.

Subha was traumatised by her son's abnormal hand and was constantly blaming herself for the defect. On a follow-up visit to the doctor, she asked him if it may have had anything to do with the medicine he'd given her for the terrible morning sickness she'd experienced. Or was it because she'd eaten something strange during the pregnancy? Was the food she ate too spicy? She had avoided the papaya and pumpkin that the ladies in the community told her not to eat, so why was she being punished?

At home, she continued to quietly fret: had there been an eclipse of the sun or the moon during her pregnancy that she hadn't been aware of? Usually, if a pregnant woman didn't take the necessary precautions during an eclipse, like refraining from the use of knives, the baby was born with a cleft palate. This wasn't just an old wives' tale, as it had happened to her sister's sister-in-law, whose son was born with a harelip. At least Ramu's face was beautiful. He had the fair complexion and light eyes of his father, and her soft features. He was adorable.

'Perhaps it is a shortcoming that he has to suffer for from his previous life?' Subha suggested to Shankar one evening, looking down at her new baby with eyes full of empathy.

Shankar nodded. 'It is the baby's own karma mingled with ours, and it is our joint responsibility to overcome this and make sure that his past sins are forgiven.'

Visitors continued to arrive. Many had heard about the 'freak' baby – as the story spread through the community, the birth defect became increasingly magnified – and had come to see him for themselves. Many wept openly on noticing the little malformed fist and could not understand a god that could be so cruel.

As with her previous recoveries, Subha relied heavily on her eldest daughter for help. Smita, often left alone to care for her new baby sibling, found him fascinating. Maybe his defect had made him more vulnerable and softened her attitude towards him, but whatever the reason, she now decided that babies were amazing; they were so tiny yet could elicit the most powerful emotions in people. They really were precious little beings.

Ramu was a soft, cuddly, gorgeous little baby who smelt wonderful and had the silkiest skin. She couldn't get enough of him; it was like having a real live doll to play with. She no longer resented changing the baby's nappies, or the residual odour of vomit that lingered on her clothes if he threw up on her. She loved it when he clasped her fingers with the tiny fingers of his normal hand.

1965: Love and culture clashes

Smita rushed towards her classroom. She couldn't wait to see all her friends again after the long summer holiday, and share the latest gossip, find out what they'd got up to during their break, and get the missing lyrics for her songbook.

She and her friends compiled all the lyrics of the latest songs they heard on the radio, then compared them, as the words were not always clear. With the new baby and the trip to Durban, the six weeks had flown by without her having had much time to be able to listen too carefully to the radio and write down all the lyrics, so she was hoping that her friends would help with filling in the blanks.

They all seemed to have the same idea. Everyone had their song books out and some of the girls were furiously copying Manju's, as she seemed to have the best ear for the lyrics. Smita was pretty good at it herself, but she struggled with some of them. Cliff Richard and the Beatles were always very clear and simple, like 'A Hard Day's Night' or 'Can't Buy Me Love', but those of the Rolling Stones and Elvis were more difficult to unravel. Some of the words made absolutely no sense.

The schoolmates had done this for many years, so were intrigued by the current songs, as well as one or two from a few years back that still made no sense. Why was there a song about a magic dragon, for instance, and what exactly were the sounds of silence? Then there were the surprises: 'My Girl' was sung by the Temptations! Smita had decided that many of the songs with more rhythm and less complex lyrics tended to be sung by black Americans, while the stranger ones were by white bands.

Smita's classmates Fatima and Roshni were not returning to school this year as their parents had decided it wasn't necessary for them to continue past their junior certificates. There was a rumour that they were either already married or were to be married shortly.

The other major news item was the new teacher, who was apparently exceedingly handsome. Smita found it difficult to associate good looks with a teacher, as most of the teachers they had were middle aged, with pot bellies from consuming too much rice and rich Indian fare without expending any calories to balance it out, but her friends insisted that she had to see this one.

'He visited us during the holiday, you know,' Manju said in a superior tone. 'He is from Durban, and he's looking for a house or a room to rent.' The focus of attention quickly shifted to her and she was assaulted with a barrage of questions. However, their enquiries had to be postponed as the siren indicating the start of the school day sounded, channelling them all to the daily assembly.

The allocation of new classrooms for the year was done, and Smita's form got the new teacher, Mr Singh, as their form master. Smita had to concede that he was indeed very handsome: he was tall and broad shouldered, and rather noble-looking, with a strong face with well-defined features, and long sideburns; his hair was brushed back just like Elvis Presley's. When he said, 'Good morning, class,' in his clipped English, his deep voice oozed confidence and charisma. It was going to be quite an exciting year.

At home, however, with the novelty of the baby having died down, things continued in the usual mundane routine. Smita had to report to the kitchen daily to either practise what she'd learnt under the critical eye of her mother, or learn new dishes. The list was endless. She'd resorted to writing many things down in a small hardcovered notebook, much to the chagrin of Subha, who said that she had all this information in her head, and hardly ever resorted to books except for when she was cooking the newer western recipes. Smita wanted to retort that her mother did not have schoolwork to contend with at the same time, but she bit her tongue.

Also, it was becoming more and more difficult to concentrate in Mr Singh's classes. He taught with such verve, and the look in his eyes revealed his passion for his subject matter. She loved it when he recited the poetry of Byron, Keats and Shakespeare, and deciphered it to reveal the magnificent meaning of the words. Why couldn't all the teachers be like that? If only she could find a man like him to marry, Smita thought. Yes, that was definitely more interesting than cooking lessons.

She did have to admit, though, that she quite liked baking from the recipes her mother cut out of the newspaper's women's page every week. Some required a creative flair. Two of her favourites were moulding dough into cone shapes, which were then filled with a scrumptious, sugary coconut mixture prior to baking, and the chocolate sandwich cookies that were filled with a delicious chocolate icing.

The Indian sweets she enjoyed making involved layers of rolled pastry that would expand into delicate, flaky boat-like shapes when fried, and which were then dipped in syrup and decorated with coloured shredded coconut – similar to the Afrikaner community's koeksisters. When Smita and her mother made these Indian sweets, Shruthi and Meera were eager to assist with the dipping into the clear bubbling syrup, and of course furtively licking their sticky fingers after they were done.

One day, Manju asked Smita to get permission from her mother to help her with some homework. Smita, glad for an excuse to be free of the drudgery of cooking, begged her mother to be allowed to go, creating an elaborate story of Manju having serious learning problems. When she got to Manju's house, another of their friends, Asha, was there as well, and Smita innocently asked if she was to tutor both of them. Asha's reply stunned her.

'We know that you read a lot, and we want some advice from you. My boyfriend is Christian and he's never going to be accepted by my family as a suitable suitor, so we want to run away. But we don't know how to go about it, and we thought you could help.'

Smita knew that if her parents found out that she was privy to this information or any runaway plan, they would crucify her. To Asha, she said, 'Why now? You have years to think about marriage. And besides, what will the two of you live on?' Then she turned to her friend. 'Manju, how can you be a part of this stupid scheme? Just think about the implications. And what will your parents say? How can you do this to them after all they have done for you?'

'Oh, please, Smita!' Manju scoffed. 'What do you know about my life? All my parents care about is their wonderful sons – who are not nearly as wonderful as they think, if they only knew what they get up to. I am the slave in the house now, having to make rotis every day after school, as my mother's back or shoulder or something is always sore. I can't wait for her to get a daughter-in-law so that she can take over—'

'And what do I need school for?' Asha interrupted. 'It is not as if we can go and carry on studying after school, because our parents don't want us to, so why should we need to finish school? Maybe I can get a job like those women in OK Bazaars and add up the money on the tills – that seems like fun!' She threw back her long black hair dramatically and said, 'Well, if no one wants to help us, maybe we will just end it all, like those two young lovers Mr Singh talked about, Romy and Julie.'

'It's Romeo and Juliet,' scolded Smita. 'You should really pay more attention when Mr Singh teaches rather than just staring at him all the time.' She didn't take Asha too seriously, as she was always making up grandiose tales and tended to live in a fantasy world.

But a few weeks later, Pitaji came home with a very grave expression on his face. He said that Asha hadn't come home from school that day, and her parents were worried sick about her.

Smita blanched and her father noticed.

'What is it, Smeets? Do you know something?'

'Well, n … not exactly, but I heard her talking about running away, b … b … but she always jokes so much and talks nonsense all the time, so I didn't think she would do something real.' Smita wailed, 'It is my fault that I did not talk her out of it!'

'Now, now. We must be calm,' her father said. 'It is not your fault although maybe you could have told us and we could have told her parents. But for now, we must just pray that she comes to her senses and returns.'

But she didn't, and Asha's parents decided that, even if she wasn't actually dead, she was certainly dead to them.

Smita recalled a story she'd heard of a girl in the remote town of Louis Trichardt who'd been involved with a supposedly low-caste boy who her parents refused to give her permission to marry, and she'd hanged herself with a sari that was supposed to be for her marriage ceremony to a suitor of the right caste chosen by her parents.

Smita had been horrified by this story. She'd been taught that if you committed suicide, your soul is never at peace and is not reincarnated and never attains moksha, or liberation from the cycle of life and death, but wanders around aimlessly forever. That thought caused shivers down her spine.

And Smita herself wasn't entirely off the hook. Whenever she ran into Asha's mother, the woman would direct horrible comments at her and swear at her under her breath – it was as if she blamed Smita for ruining her daughter's life and consequently their reputation as a family.

Asha's antics caused a wide ripple effect. Some parents, panicking about their daughters' exposure to 'western novels' that were putting ideas into their heads, removed them from the school. Some were so incensed they even wanted to get rid of Mr Singh, as they thought that the English novels he encouraged the girls to read influenced them into believing in love marriages and not following tradition.

Subha, in the meantime, quickly tasked her matchmaking networks of sisters and cousins with finding a suitable match for Smita as soon as they could. She would just convince Shankar that if they did not want their daughter to disappear with some riffraff, he would have to acquiesce to her wishes.

Months later, a rumour did the rounds that Asha and her paramour had gone off to Rhodesia, where the Christian boy had relatives who were running a missionary school, and that they were living quite happily running a general dealer's shop near the church. But no one knew for sure.

1965: Rejection and regret

The thunder pealed through the skies, accompanied by the spectacular lightning show typical of a highveld storm. It felt as if the house was shuddering with the impact. Smita generally loved watching these storms, and the sounds and smells that accompanied them – the pitter-patter of the first raindrops and the amazing olfactory sensations they provoked after a long hot summer's day's dust settled on the roads – but today she sat alone in the dark, ignoring the rain, her own tears splashing onto her homemade cotton summer nightdress. She tried not to make any noise, as the rest of the household was asleep, and muffled the sounds of her sobbing by biting into her blanket. The worst part was that in her heart she knew that she should be happy, as she'd escaped what would have been a disaster – but rejection was a bitter pill to swallow, especially since she'd been convinced that he would be smitten by her.

When her mother had first told her that these people were coincidentally visiting some other relatives nearby, and that they were just stopping by to introduce their son to the family, merely to see if it might work out in the future, Smita had allowed herself to be swept away by the excitement.

At the first meeting, Ajay was initially reserved and didn't want to make eye contact; later, though, when the two of them went into the back yard and left their parents talking, he looked at her and grinned. 'Hey, I remember you from Durban – Rani's wedding. You and Rupa were up on the balcony, peering through the balustrades at me.'

Smita remembered the day clearly – Ajay was the winking boy! He'd performed some amazing tricks with the soccer ball, heading it for longer than she'd seen anyone do before, and even tapping it with one foot multiple times, after which he'd deftly kicked it with his heel and caught it on his foot again. She and Rupa had been in awe of his talent, and had applauded, and he'd looked up at them with this same mischievous grin.

Now, as the two of them stood together self-consciously outside, she tried to ignore his thick lips and slightly pockmarked face, and focus instead on his thick dark curly hair and animated expression when talking about his love for soccer, which had persisted through the years. He now played soccer professionally, for Durban United. The Natal league had just recently joined the Transvaal and Cape football leagues to form the South African players' football league, which consisted of all non-white players, he told her.

Playing soccer meant he got to travel, he said, enabling him to explore parts of the country that he would not ordinarily have visited, and meet the different kinds of people of South Africa. He excitedly explained how interesting it was to visit the homes of some of the Malay players in Cape Town. She was thrilled by Ajay's wonderful stories, and impressed by the fact that he'd seen Table Mountain, that really, he said, did have a flat top like a table.

There was even the shocking story of how they'd almost got arrested en route to the Cape in the Orange Free State. Indians weren't allowed access to that province without a permit. They were also not permitted to stay the night. The organisers had followed due process and obtained permits for the time they thought it would take to travel through the area en route to Cape Town.

They were unlucky, though, and the bus got a flat tyre right in the middle of the province. This took some time to sort out, and many of the players took advantage of the stop to eat, stretch their legs and relax a bit. Some policemen in a passing patrol car demanded to see their permits; the cops had obviously thought that it was a great opportunity to bully a couple of coolies. The team manager was obsequious – 'Ja, baas, so sorry, baas, ons is baie jammer' – which seemed to mollify the policemen, and when he surreptitiously handed them some money, they let the players go on their way with a stern warning not to make any other stops.

The road trips Ajay's team went on were almost beyond Smita's imagination: sleeping on the side of the road, as there were few hotels for 'non-whites', and getting your blanket blown away by passing lorries; having to eat cold tinned beans on bread, as no restaurant would serve them and they did not have any way of warming the food ... it seemed like a western movie!

He'd led such an eventful life so far, and she didn't blame him for not wanting to join his father's bus company and drive buses the whole day when he could be playing soccer all over the country. She was certainly fascinated by his life, and that alone did create some degree of attraction.

The tea was served on Ma's best crockery – a wedding gift, it only made an appearance when there were very important guests to entertain. The pieces were all bordered with gold paint on the fluted edges and had small flowers painted on them.

The next morning, at the breakfast table, Subha and Shankar told Smita that Ajay's parents had found her pretty, and that they wanted to confirm the proposal in a few months' time. Ajay had said that she could write to him, but as he was busy playing soccer, his replies would be irregular and unreliable.

'So, you are happy then, Smita?' her mother asked. 'He looks like a nice boy, not too fat and quite fair, so you will have fair children, and you know what a big house they have in Durban. Imagine you staying like a maharani there! Only thing is, they do eat meat, but you can learn to cook it, my dear. So, don't disappoint me now, just say you like him too.' Subha stared hard at her eldest daughter, a fixed smile on her face.

Smita, overwhelmed by how fast everything was moving, felt tears stinging her eyes. She'd been hoping for a few more meetings with Ajay but she knew that because they lived in the Transvaal and his home was in Natal, this would be difficult.

Her father, noting Smita's expression, smiled gently and said to his wife, 'Don't force her. Let her think about it.'

'You are too soft!' Ma snapped. 'They want an answer so they can tell their family about it, and we have to start planning the engagement party. You know, they are rich people—'

'Okay, Ma,' Smita said quickly. She didn't want to sit through another of her mother's lectures.

'That's my girl!' Subha said, beaming from ear to ear.

೮ ೧

The next few months passed as in a dream. Smita confided in Mariam, as she too was promised to someone – with Muslim girls this practice seemed much more common. But she could not bring herself to confess to any of her other friends that she had succumbed to her parents' wishes and was not pursuing any further education. Being one of the students who constantly excelled in tests and examinations, it was simply expected that she would be studying further.

She often caught herself staring at some of the boys in her class, especially Arvind, whom all the girls likened to the Bollywood heart throb Raj Kapoor. His features were perfect, with a sculpted face, dreamy expressive eyes and a beautiful smile. Most of the girls hoped that he would send some affection in their direction but they knew he only had eyes for Smita.

One afternoon, after netball practice, he approached her coyly and motioned her towards the back of the changing rooms. She thought he wanted to ask her something about their English homework, as he never paid attention in class, but instead, talking quickly in a strange voice, he said, 'Smita, you are the most gorgeous girl in this school. I cannot stop thinking about you – your laugh, your beautiful smile – and I think that I am utterly and hopelessly in love with you. It is all in there,' and he pressed something into her hand and briskly walked away.

Smita, her cheeks burning, looked down – it was a letter.

She could not believe what had just transpired. She ran home with her heart racing and almost forgot to conceal the note in the pocket of her dress as she rushed into the kitchen.

Later, when she read Arvind's letter, her chest constricted, and it seemed that her heart was breaking into a million pieces. He wrote that he thought they were meant for each other, and that she was his soulmate; he wanted to spend the rest of his life with her and could not imagine an existence without her.

She sobbed unashamedly into her pillow, for him and for herself and for the ruination of her life. If only she could marry him instead of being forced to marry a man she hardly knew, and who had interests so different from hers, and who had so much worldly experience! She'd known Arvind all her life, and she could talk to him and laugh with him, and she knew that she wouldn't mind looking at him every day when she woke up in the mornings – even though looks weren't supposed to be the deciding criterion when choosing a husband, or so her mother insisted. Well, it was easy for her to say: Pitaji was very good looking.

She thought about the Shakespearean sonnet the class had just learnt: 'Let me not to the marriage of true minds admit impediments ...' It personified her feelings for Arvind. She was sure that they would have a marriage where love would 'not alter when it alteration finds'. However, she knew it could never be: Arvind's family came from a much lower caste – his family were banyas, a merchant class – and from a very early age she'd been made painfully aware that a prerequisite for a match was that any prospective husband be from a Brahmin family.

Finally, Smita decided that she would reply to Arvind in a letter and tell him all her problems. He had to understand.

She wasn't sure if she'd clarified all she needed to in the letter, but she tried as best she could to explain what her parents wanted, and that she couldn't simply indulge her own selfish feelings.

His reaction was worrying. Catching her between classes a few days later, he pulled her aside and said in an urgent voice, 'I don't think that I can bear to live without you. Why don't we run away together, Smita?'

While Smita, panicked and tearful, tried to find an answer, Arvind continued, 'We can start a new life somewhere, just the two of us. I have relatives in England who won't throw me out. They're more liberated there than our parents here. And we could get jobs, and study part time. It will be so wonderful to start anew somewhere else, rather than continue living in this backwater town.'

The days that followed were like she was waiting for someone to shake her from a nightmare. She didn't want to have the party to finalise the proposal from Ajay – she was far from convinced that Ajay was 'the one' – but Ma was so thrilled at the prospect, and he was from such an affluent family, and she would get to move to Durban and away from this sleepy town ... And he wasn't that unattractive – at least he wasn't shorter than her, which was a fear she'd secretly harboured as she'd grown progressively taller. Although Smita loved being tall, and knew that in the western world all the models who graced the covers of the magazines were tall and slender, about a year before, she'd overheard a meddling aunt tell her mother, 'This girl is shooting up too much, Subha. I hope you will find a boy for her. You know, men do not want to be looking up at their wives.'

And then came the bombshell. A letter arrived from Ajay, informing her that he 'regretfully could not go through with the engagement party' as he had proposed to someone else.

As Smita stood staring uncomprehendingly at the letter, her mother fluttered around her, trilling, 'So, when are they coming? How many people will be coming for the party? We have so much to do – we need to decide what you are going to wear, what we will cook, what sweets to make—'

'Ma, please! He is calling it off!' Smita choked.

The look of shock and disappointment on Subha's face was enough to cause Smita to burst into tears. She ran out the back door and took refuge under the peach tree, where she sat bent over her knees, sobbing relentlessly onto her school dress. She knew that deep down she did not want to have an arranged marriage; she had been so against it from the beginning. But to be rejected was an entirely new feeling for her. It was so humiliating.

She couldn't understand it. Ajay had seemed to like her. Everyone always told her how pretty she was and she herself knew there was some truth to this. She was never arrogant but when she compared herself to her friends, she would have been blind not to have noticed that she had flawless skin, a nose that was neither too long nor stubby, and nice eyes with long eyelashes. So what was the problem? Maybe she was too immature for him. Or had she offended him in some way?

She bit the hem of her dress and screamed through her teeth in frustration, which made her feel a bit better. At least now maybe Ma would ease off with her efforts to find a suitable boy. She would concentrate on school and enjoy the time with her family. There was so much more to life than getting married.

Subha, obviously worried about her daughter, surreptitiously peeped through the window overlooking the garden. She was also bitterly disappointed with Ajay and his family. How could his parents have brought him up so badly? Did they not tell him that he was supposed to get married to a girl from a good family and not run after any passing skirt? She had heard the rumours about the coloured girl he was seeing but had chosen to ignore them, thinking that once he was engaged to her beautiful Smita, he would forget about this other girl and come to his senses.

As much as she scolded her eldest daughter, Subha was very proud of her beauty. She was coming along nicely in the kitchen too.

Subha shook her head and clicked her tongue. No matter about Ajay. They must just forget him. The perfect match would come along very soon.

ॐ ༀ

Smita was still tired after a troubled night as she walked into the classroom the next day. She was late again, as she'd had to comb and plait her sisters' hair and help them get ready for the day, then help Ma make the sandwiches for the morning break at school. All three girls were now at school, so that meant making at least six sandwiches daily, or more, if they had to attend later lessons or sport practice in the afternoon. Subha had relented and allowed Smita to use shop-brought bread – the effort of baking bread was just too much for her, on top of everything she had to do for her growing family. It was only Pitaji's lunch that generally contained homemade bread or roti.

The class was abuzz with excitement, which Smita thought was enthusiasm for the much-anticipated sports day that lay ahead. But then she overheard a classmate say, 'Imagine quiet little Harsha as a teacher – the students would all run amok!' Someone else said, 'But if it was Mohammed, they would be terrified.' 'What about Yusuf as a lawyer – he already thinks he is one, he talks so much!' came a third voice, and everyone giggled.

Smita went over to the noisy bunch gathered around the teacher's desk. There were at least a dozen colourful brochures spread out there, which the pupils were looking over. The leaflets contained info about possible jobs for school-leavers.

'Hey, Smita, what would you like to be when we leave this dump?' asked Teju, the loudest mouth in the class.

'You'll be a BSc, Teju,' one of his friends teased him. 'BSc' referred not to a science degree, but to 'behind shop counter', the fate for many of the youngsters who wouldn't be able to get into university.

'It's the lucky ones like Arvind who'll go overseas to become doctors,' one of the girls noted, smiling up the handsome youngster. 'Right, Arvind?'

Smita glanced over at Arvind, who quickly looked away from her. Was he really going overseas to study? This was news to her. Arvind's family owned the local general dealers, basically a fruit and vegetable shop, so he would really be breaking the mould if he became a doctor.

Quelling her feelings of disappointment that Arvind hadn't confided in her, Smita looked over the brochures on the desk. The one with the picture of the pretty young nurse with a huge smile, kitted out in a pristine white uniform with a little gold watch pinned to it, caught her eye. 'Is studying nursing for you?' the caption read.

She slipped it out of the pile and paged through it. The idea of caring for people did greatly appeal to her, and although she felt that teaching may be a more glamorous profession, the sense of accomplishment from assisting someone to get well would probably, she thought, be more fulfilling than screaming at a bunch of ungrateful children. Maybe she could be like Florence Nightingale – then there would be no need to get married, as she would serve the community. In Hinduism, service to man was a very important duty to fulfil. Surely her parents could not object if this noble profession was her chosen path?

As it turned out, they could object, and they did – or at least her mother did. 'What? You want to do that dirty job?' Subha raged when Smita raised the subject with her that afternoon after school.

'You think I raised you to go clean other people's bedpans? That is not the work of a Brahmin girl! Have you totally lost your mind? I told your father you should have left school long ago and stayed here at home to help me! Instead, he thinks it is good for you to carry on and finish. For what purpose? Here I am trying so hard to find one nice rich match for you so you can be a good housewife and you want to think about working!'

Subha stared angrily at her daughter, who stared angrily back. 'There are still so many things that you don't know. It is also all these stupid books you read, and the silly songs on that radio you stick your ears on.'

Subha turned away from Smita, attacking the sinkful of dishes with furious energy. 'I am quite fed up now,' she said over her shoulder. 'You think you can be like a gora in those books? Hmpf! Your father will have to put you in your place. If it was up to me, I think you should just leave school now. No one cares whether a girl finished matric when they want her for a wife. Who worries about that? All they want to know is if you are pretty enough and healthy enough, and that you can cook, do housework and look after your mother-in-law. After all the years of bringing up children, the mother-in-law deserves a rest.'

Subha yanked her hands out of the suds and turned back to Smita. 'This why I am glad that I have sons now, so that I will have two daughters-in-law to look after me when I am old. After looking after all of you children for all these years, I will deserve a good daughter-in-law to care for me.'

Smita felt this reference to her brothers was unfair: she had helped her mother clean the house and cook for the family since she was young, and, of course, she'd looked after her numerous younger siblings. For most Indian girls, including the daughters-in-law that Subha saw in her future, that vicious cycle would almost certainly continue into adulthood: forced into marriage at a young age, they would produce babies that they were probably not emotionally ready for, and be a source of cheap labour for their husband's extended family, cooking and cleaning for them.

Putting her soapy hands on her hips and looking accusingly at Smita, Subha asked, 'And if you go to work after you are married, who will look after your children? Your in-laws? You expect a mother-in-law to look after your children while you are gallivanting around, worrying about the world? And you know nurses work night shifts? Which man will ever want to be married to you if you are not there to warm his bed at night?'

Smita, her anger giving way to dismay, was close to tears after this onslaught from her mother – but then she realised that she should not have expected anything different. Just the other day, she'd overheard Pitaji telling Ma about a new young woman on his staff. She was from a well-respected North Indian Brahmin family and the only daughter. All her brothers had been to college, so her father had decided that she should be educated as well. But while she was at teacher-training college, she'd met and fallen in love with a Tamil fellow, and had insisted on marrying him when she qualified. This was a worse transgression than marrying out of caste. Tamils were of South Indian origin, and how could a woman from a North Indian Hindi-speaking family marry into this family? It was just not done. There were differences in the cultural beliefs, traditions and practices that were not understood by the other side and were regarded with disdain.

Obviously, this had not gone down well with her family, Pitaji told Ma, but her father finally had no choice but to accede. So there she was now, as Mrs Naidoo and teaching at school where her father taught as well. Smita did not know the teachers at his school so she had no idea who this poor woman was, but she felt bad for her.

Ma, who'd made disapproving 'tut-tut' noises throughout the telling of this story, looked positively scandalised when Pitaji added that Mrs Naidoo had a little son who she left in the care of her mother-in-law.

'Well, it's better than leaving him with a nanny girl, but imagine her poor mother-in-law, who needs her daughter-in-law to care for her, and now has to care for her grandchildren!' Subha huffed. She had strong feelings about children being left with African maids: 'They tie the children on their backs so that they can finish the housework! What nonsense is this? The child the whole day on the back of a maid? And who knows what they feed the children? I've heard stories of maids who give these children their breasts to suckle on! Can you imagine that!'

Smita felt her fighting spirit was defeated, and that she now had no choice but to quietly accept the fate that was sure to befall her soon.

∽ ∾

The second half of the year was always an eventful time on the Hindu calendar. It started with a period that was considered inauspicious, so time was dedicated to paying obeisance to the ancestors. There was a lot of superstition about the dead and it was believed that during this period, the souls of the departed came visiting the family. Prayers were done to please the ancestors and ask for forgiveness for any wrongdoing against them. Weddings, birthday parties and other celebrations were not allowed during this time.

This was followed by the exciting festival of Navaratri, nine nights to commemorate the Hindu pantheon of goddesses. The goddesses were represented as different forms for the various gifts that they were supposed to bestow, not unlike the fairies in the children's story *Sleeping Beauty*: Saraswathi was worshipped for wealth of wisdom and education, for example, Lakshmi for financial prosperity and Kali to destroy all evil. A ritual was performed solely by married women for the various goddesses, which Smita had to learn, and this required the preparation of a flour-based thick pudding called halwa, encased in little fried breads. This prayer was also done by a mother of a child at the end of some contagious illness, to appease the divine mother and implore her not to inflict the illness again, and to thank her for the recovery of the child.

The Gujarati community performed garba dances in praise of the female goddesses at the local hall. Smita and Shruthi, who were now eighteen and fourteen, were allowed to attend these folk dances, in which the women and girls clapped hands and went around in a circle, joined later by the men and boys sporting wooden sticks called dandiyas. And this was where Smita and Arvind found themselves next to each other.

Arvind had evidently not taken Smita's rejection well, and it had been distressing for her to see him at school every day and not be able to talk to him, as they really had been good friends and she'd once been able to confide in him. She'd loved talking to him about the books they were reading, and now she had no one to talk to about *Tess of the d'Urbervilles*, the Thomas Hardy novel that wrenched her heart. It seemed the fate of women all over the world to suffer.

Now, as the dancing and singing grew more frenzied, she felt her arm being urgently pulled, and Arvind dragged her into the little room next to the stage that was used as a dressing room for concerts and by brides when they needed to change saris during the wedding ceremonies that took place here from time to time.

'Are you insane? Someone will see!' Smita hissed, although her heart was pounding from excitement. She could not believe that he could be so brazen – but also so thoughtless. Didn't he care for her reputation?

'Why won't you talk to me any more?' Arvind asked urgently, holding Smita by both upper arms and staring intensely into her eyes. 'Oh, my beautiful Smita, I miss you so much, my heart breaks whenever I see you.' Letting go of her arms, he moved his hands up to her face and held it in his two soft palms. 'If nothing else, at least we have this moment that we can always remember,' he said, then drew her close to him and kissed her passionately on the lips for what seemed like an eternity.

When he finally, gently, disengaged from her, she felt so breathless she thought she might faint. Her head was spinning. Had she really just experienced her first kiss? The earth had not exactly moved for her; in fact, it had been a little overwhelming for her and she wasn't sure that she'd enjoyed it. But she did feel exhilaration that Arvind felt so strongly about her. Still, the thought of her parents finding out filled her with dread; they would think she was such a disappointment for having allowed this to happen. Her mother especially would probably deprecate her for being a degenerate. She knew how Subha loved to exaggerate.

Not realising what a welter of emotions was welling up in Smita, Arvind said, 'Just remember, Smita, that I love you and will never love anyone else as much.' Then, after giving her hands a reassuring squeeze, he turned and left the little room.

Smita stood there for a few moments, excited and fearful, but most of all confused. She'd thought she had got over her infatuation with Arvind, and that she missed his friendship more than anything else; and she wondered if what she was feeling was just because she too wanted the intense passion felt by the heroines in the books she read, or if the thrill of the incident stemmed from its clandestine nature and the fact that it was her first real kiss, rather than being in love.

ಋ 12 ಞ

1966: Another suitable boy

Today was to be an interesting day, following some months of boredom and stress. The final matriculation exams had been predictably difficult, and Smita had not had as much time as she would have liked to spend on her studies. She had, however, managed to achieve above-average results for her senior certificate, which had permitted her entrance into university – not that she had applied to any, given the vociferous objections of her mother whenever she dared mention the subject.

Still, Smita continued to hope that her mother wouldn't be able to find a suitable match for her, and that Subha would finally accept that her daughter was condemned to spinsterhood, and therefore had to find some way of supporting herself financially and give in and allow her to go to university for further studies.

At the same time, Smita's domestic duties had not diminished at all. It was as if Subha was trying to impress on her that she did not need to excel at school, as being a housewife and mother had no academic entry requirements.

But today could take Smita's life in a whole new direction and, in spite of herself, she was excited. She glanced at her reflection through the ethereal haze in the bathroom. The steam created while she'd filled the bath was luxuriously warm and comforting. She dipped in a toe to feel the temperature – perfect – and slowly lowered herself into the welcoming water. As she submerged her body in the bath, it felt like she was indulging in some decadently forbidden activity. The girls were repeatedly warned by the father about not using too much hot water – Pitaji claimed that the electricity bill was being hugely elevated by the new electric geyser which magically supplied boiling water right out of the tap. Previously the electricity bill had been for the lights and the refrigerator, but now, with the electric stove and the geyser, it was becoming ridiculous, according to Shankar.

While Pitaji would have been happy for the household to continue heating water for washing on one side of the coal stove while the other side was used for cooking, Ma had complained that she was tired of hauling heavy tubs of water back and forth. And when some of the scalding water she was carrying slopped out of the tub and splashed onto Ramu's feet, she became incandescent with rage at her husband. 'It could have been so much worse, and all because of your miserliness! I cannot believe that you would sacrifice your child's life to save a few rands! What kind of father are you? What would you do with the money if he got burns all over and died?'

Ramu had not been seriously injured – the splashes of boiling water had raised two small blisters on one of his feet, which had soon healed – but despite the histrionic exaggerations of his wife, Shankar relented. At first he himself would not use the geyser, just to try to make a point, and he persisted in heating his water on the stove, but eventually even he succumbed to the convenience and comfort.

As Smita languished in the hot scented water, she thought about Ma and how ecstatic she'd been since this latest potential suitor had been found. Virat, who was living with his parents in Stanger, a small town on the Natal north coast, was in the process of completing a post-graduate degree in law through the University of South

Africa. His parents had thought it would be a wonderful idea for them to visit their old friend, Shankar, and for their son to meet one of Shankar's lovely daughters. Shankar and Virat's father, Mr Sharma, had studied teaching together and occasionally met at various family weddings.

When Shankar had told Subha about the impending visit, she was beside herself with elation. The parents were not very rich but they had good standing in their community – the father was a well-known school principal – and they were of the right caste. She immediately put out word on the Durban grapevine, and learnt that Virat had already turned down many pretty girls, as he was too busy with his studies to give attention to choosing a wife. Subha was hopeful that her Smita would be more successful than the others.

Climbing out the bath and reaching for a towel to begin the laborious task of drying her long hair, Smita thought enviously of Miss Samuel's latest hairstyle, which was the fashionable bob. But Ma made her girls care for their hair carefully, not allowing them to cut it shorter, and applying a blend of coconut, almond and olive oils every weekend so that it was soft and shiny. Even if the smell of the coconut oil permeated the pillows you slept on, and it was quite a mission to get the smell out of your hair, it did seem to have a beneficial effect, as Smita and her sisters had stunning hair.

She selected an exquisite burnt-orange sari to wear for the day that perfectly complemented her flawless, creamy complexion – a real peaches-and-cream combination. Subha had acquired an impressive collection of saris over the years that she did not wear often, and Smita had been allowed to choose from these for this special occasion.

When she went through to the kitchen to help Subha finish plating all the snacks she'd spent the morning making, despite her sisters' admiring looks and her mother's praise, Smita felt nervous. If Virat was so interested in his studies and not interested in other girls, why would he be interested in her? And did she have the strength to handle another rejection? Her mother's faith in her was strong but she herself did not feel that confident.

Virat and his family finally arrived. Smita's parents welcomed them into the lounge and occupied themselves with the mandatory small talk while her sisters peeped through the slightly open door and reported back to Smita, who sat on in her bedroom, too anxious to join in their spying.

'He's quite good looking – not like that previous one with the thick lips and the big nose,' Shruthi giggled.

'Maybe his ears stick out a bit too much,' Meera offered. 'He is fair, though – that will make Ma happy.'

Finally, Smita was summoned. On legs that felt weak, she tentatively entered the room, too nervous to look at anyone directly.

'This is Mr and Mrs Sharma, and their son, Virat,' she heard Shankar saying. 'This is our daughter, Smita.'

Smita, her heart jumping and nerves trapping her tongue, stood still and silent, like a statue.

'Please greet our guests, Smita, then you can have a seat,' her father ordered gently.

Smita's heart sank. Now they would think she was an absolute imbecile who didn't have any manners and could not even speak without being prompted. Stammering greetings, she felt around behind her for a chair and, mightily relieved, sat down. While the conversation started up again, she sneaked a peek at her suitor. His name, she remembered, meant 'majestic and brilliant', and he did indeed look quite majestic, with broad shoulders and his chest puffed out, and sitting upright with his hands on his knees.

Just then he glanced sideways and caught her eye, and his expression of excruciated embarrassment made her register that her own Prince Charming was finding this all as uncomfortable and awkward as she was. Feeling somewhat mollified by this realisation, she glanced at his parents. His mother, who was wearing a pretty sari of an unusual colour, smiled warmly at her, and his father, a tall broad-shouldered man with kind grey eyes and an amiable look, said, 'Well, let us include the youngsters in the conversation.' Turning to Smita, he continued, 'What grade have you finished in school?'

'I've just got my senior certificate,' Smita replied, shyly.

Mr Sharma raised his eyebrows in approval. 'It is commendable that your mother and father are broadminded enough to allow you to finish school. Not all Indian girls are so lucky.'

Subha, cringing inwardly and feeling her cheeks burning, glanced at Shankar, who simply nodded and refused to look at her. Subha then broke the tension in the room by clapping her hands and saying, 'Tea time! Come, Smita, help me in the kitchen.'

Only too relieved to be able to escape the keyed-up atmosphere in the front room, Smita obediently followed her mother to the kitchen, where Subha was already muttering angrily under her breath. 'Hmpf! They've got a cheek, telling us what is good for our children. If he was not so goodlooking, I would not be interested. At least now you can have fair children as well as clever ones, but hopefully they won't be daughters. What is the use of clever daughters anyway? They all have to get married in the end!'

Smita focused on filling the milk jug and the sugar bowl, while her mother made the tea.

'The tea has to be strong so that they know we are giving them quality, not the cheap dishwater that some people serve,' Subha said. 'You just go put the cups on the tray.'

The crockery was again the best set, kept for special occasions, with little delicate gold-rimmed cups and saucers. Carefully, with trembling hands, Smita stacked everything on the tray and carried it through to their guests.

While Subha poured and handed around cups of strong tea, Smita stole another glance at Virat, only to find him looking at her. Her heart leapt into her throat and she felt the blood rush to her face.

'Smita seems to be a bit hot in that sari!' her prospective father-in-law boomed, noticing her burning cheeks. 'Virat, maybe you need to take her outside to the veranda for a bit. I am sure she is not used to wearing saris and whatnot in this weather.'

Smita heard the suppressed giggles from her sisters and she knew that they were highly amused at the way this man spoke, the way he enunciated his words and said 'veranda' when they called it a stoep; where did these people come from – England?

Outside, Smita was able to examine her prospective fiancé more closely. He was a very attractive man, taller than her, with an angular, clean-shaven face, perfectly sculpted cheekbones, kind, expressive eyes and a softly spoken manner. Was this her Mr Rochester? Or her Heathcliff? No, Heathcliff was too tragic. He was probably more like Mr Darcy.

They both sat down gratefully in the wicker armchairs. He smiled at her and a flock of butterflies immediately took flight in her stomach. Was this what it was supposed to feel like? The feelings described in the poems and the books?

'What are your hobbies, Smita? Do you like books? Do you keep up with current affairs, world politics, the Vietnam war in America, the recent advances in space travel?'

Although the battery of questions were delivered in Virat's gentle voice, immediately the anxieties set in. What if this was a test of some kind, to make sure she wasn't just eye candy? What if he didn't like how she answered? Maybe he thought she was just a silly, frivolous creature, able only to read and write at a basic level, and wanting just to marry and procreate.

Smiling, she deflected the spotlight back onto him. 'I hear you are studying law,' she said. 'Is it interesting?'

'Yes, and I hope to emulate the great lawyers in history once I've graduated.'

'Like Gandhi and Nehru, you mean?' she asked, a modest demonstration of her knowledge.

'Yes, and our own lawyers here, the great Nelson Mandela and Oliver Tambo, fighting for equal rights and freedom for all South Africans,' Virat said, fervently, leaning forward in the chair and staring straight into Smita's eyes. Then, his tone softening, he reached out and took one of her hands. 'Smita, I am so glad I travelled here to meet you. We have so little time, so I just want you to know, as much as my rational brain does not believe in fate, it does seem that we were fated to meet. I cannot explain it, but your presence has this effect on me, and it is not just your beauty. It is all quite uncanny. I would love to write to you and express myself properly, as I am quite overwhelmed now.'

Once again, the blood rushed up into Smita's cheeks, but she managed to blurt out, 'I would like that, Virat.'

At that moment, Shankar came and called them inside, and the rest of the afternoon passed in a blur, with Smita and Virat exchanging a couple of quick glances and smiles.

Could it be this simple, that was he the one? Smita thought. She could certainly spend her life looking into those eyes and waking up to that smile every day. As the realisation dawned that what she wanted to do, in fact, was jump up and down and scream with glee, it suddenly made sense to her why the heroes and heroines of Hindi movies broke out into song when they were happy. She felt like she could do that too.

In the days after Virat's visit, Smita recalled his every word, and would often find herself staring dreamily into space. She kept an eye on the postbox at the end of the short front-garden path, waiting for the postman to arrive, and then running out in expectation as soon as he'd put the family's mail in the box and walked on.

Her sisters teased her relentlessly, but also expressed some of their misgivings. 'I think we are going to have a new brother-in-law but you will move so far away,' said Meera. 'What will we do without you?'

'Yes, and the baby is so attached to you, he will probably cry every day,' Shruthi added.

As if on cue, baby Ramu crawled quickly over to them – he'd adapted almost seamlessly to his deformed hand, and it didn't slow him down at all. Pulling himself up on his eldest sister's legs, he held out his arms, indicating that she should pick him up. Smita was glad for the distraction.

A letter finally arrived a week later. Smita put it in her pocket and waited until her curious siblings were distracted, then went outside and sat under the peach tree to read it.

Dearest Smita, the letter began, in a well-formed, flowing script.

I do hope that this letter finds you and your wonderful family in good health.

As you may know, our rendezvous was suggested by one of the matchmakers (aka busybodies) of the family, as he had seen you and thought you would make an excellent match for me. He reminded my father of his friend from college – your father – and mentioned that this friend had a daughter.

Various busybodies have arranged many such meetings for me – at the age of 26, and a lawyer in training, I suppose I am considered ideal husband material. None of these meetings has been a success for me. However, when I saw you, I was mesmerised. I was captivated by your elegant height, the grace with which you carried yourself, and, of course, your beautiful face with its perfect features. But beyond your alluring appeal, there was something about you that was an instantaneous attraction that I cannot explain. Normally I am a focused, rational person but meeting you has changed that. I feel, as ridiculous as it might seem, that our souls are destined to be entwined together for seven lives, as is written in the scriptures.

I hope you do not think that I have taken leave of my

senses, and that being honest with you in this way will not
scare you off – but I had to tell you how I feel, and I need
to know if you feel the same.

When it comes to practicalities, if we should decide to
pursue this relationship, you do need to know that I have
just completed my degree and in the first few years I will
not be earning too much. Your father's house is luxurious,
and the furnishings are all very fancy, and I want to warn
you that I cannot promise you this. My parents' house is
modest, so you would need to adjust to these changes.

I await your reply and I am hoping that it will be positive.
Best wishes
Virat

In the days following the receipt of Virat's letter, Smita had a smile
frozen on her face and was in a constant dreamlike state. She knew
that Virat would be waiting for a reply, and she would have to sit
down and write one soon, but her anxiety that she would not be as
eloquent as him bothered her. And while he professed to have been
honest about how he felt about her, she wasn't sure how transparent
she should be about her own feelings.

Subha, whom Smita had kept in ignorance about the receipt of the
letter, did not leave her in peace either. 'Smita, what did you think of
that nice young man? I am sure he enjoyed the tea that we put out.
I made sure that I told his mother what a good cook you are, just so
they know my daughters are not lazy and are very capable. He
seemed happy when he left here.'

Smita turned away and rolled her eyes. She was pretty certain that
the last thing on Virat's mind was her cooking.

Her mother rabbited on. 'Cat got your tongue? Are you going to
marry this fellow or not? We cannot keep asking people to come
here to see you, you know. We—'

'Ma! I like him. I think I can marry him.'

There was a stunned silence before a genuinely happy if somewhat self-satisfied grin spread across Subha's face. 'Well, you had better tell him, then,' she said, now all business. 'You cannot keep him waiting and we will need to start making all the arrangements.' Then her facial features softened, and in a rare show of maternal affection, she reached out and pulled Smita to her, hugging her tightly. 'I am so relieved, my dearest Smeets. We will be having a wedding now.' Pushing Smita gently away from herself, she held her eldest daughter by the upper arms and looked her up and down. 'Where did the years go, Smita? I have been so busy with all these children and here you are, all grown up.'

Now that the cat was out of the bag, Smita decided she had to write to Virat before her mother began interfering. Lying tummy-down on her bed, and using a sheet of school notebook paper, she wrote:

Dear Virat,

Thank you for your letter. I hope that you and your family are well too.

I was really happy to receive your letter and I am so glad that we feel the same way. You seem like a wonderful person and I do like you, so I have told my mother that we can continue to meet.

I also got a sense that we are destined for each other, and somehow there is a feeling of familiarity or comfort, like I have known you forever. It is all a little strange and I do not really believe in fate and the seven lives that you mentioned but I cannot explain the feelings any other way.

Sorry that I cannot be as eloquent as you but I am looking forward to reading your next letter.

Regards

Smita

She dearly wanted to say more, to tell him how attractive she found him, and that for her it was love at first sight, but she just could not do it. She hoped that he would read between the lines and understand her and realise that she was shy.

After she posted the letter, more torturous days followed while she waited for a reply. Fortunately, however, there was a new distraction for her around this time, in the form of Sunita, a young woman from Kenya who had recently married a distant cousin, Kirit, who lived in the neighbourhood, and whose proud mother visited frequently with her new daughter-in-law.

Sunita at nineteen was near in age to Smita, and Smita was fascinated by the young bride. She was flawlessly beautiful, and Smita thought that it was a pity that she had to be married to Kirit, who was not the most attractive, although he obviously adored his new wife.

At the age of fifteen, Sunita had been orphaned during the uprising in Kenya. The Kenyan Land and Freedom Army, known as the Mau Mau, had fought for independence from the British for many years, and had finally succeeded in 1960. The new regime in Kenya had wanted Indians living in the country to relinquish their Indian citizenship or British citizenship and solely retain Kenyan citizenship. The Indians who refused were seen as traitors, leading to violent attacks on them and their businesses. It was a small mercy that on the terrible morning Sunita's family's shop had been looted and her mother and father cruelly killed, she had been at school.

Sunita had been left in the care of an uncle and aunt who had planned to go to England to escape the new government in Kenya. Most of their compatriots who'd gone to England had had to accept lower-paying jobs, so Sunita's uncle did not want the burden of Sunita being financially dependent on him. He thought that the best decision was for her to be married before he and his wife emigrated, and was only too relieved when family living in South Africa helped to connect him with Kirit's parents.

Sunita regaled Smita and her sisters with stories of her life in Kenya which, she said, was a lot like South Africa except that there were no Afrikaners; it was just another British colony. Most of the Indians who lived there had initially been brought over as cheap labour to work on the railway lines: about 30 000 Indians were recruited as indentured labourers from 1896, and most had stayed on. Many of those who stayed became railway officials or businessmen. There was, however, a lot of discontent in the country, Sunita said, as Indians were perceived to be corrupt and thieving businessmen who preyed on the fiscal ignorance of the masses and accumulated their wealth in this manner.

Sunita told Smita of her troubles with calm and the ease of someone narrating a story about a stranger, but Smita could see the pain in her eyes when she described her beautiful mother who had come from India to marry her father, and how her mother had never really adapted to Kenya but had tolerated it because she was a dutiful Indian wife.

Sunita herself had loved Kenya, and said that there was to a certain extent a camaraderie there between the races that was not present in South Africa. They were aware of the differences but in Kenya you could play with white and black children on the streets, and it was never a big issue.

She was also shocked at the divisions in the Indian community in Bakerton. In Kenya, she said, everyone respected each other's religions, and when it came to celebrations like Diwali and Eid, the families all got together for feasts, and everyone loved getting dressed up in their finery for these occasions. In South Africa, she observed, it seemed that Muslims were quite isolated, and that while Hindu and Muslim children seemed to socialise at school, this did not carry into households at home.

'Maybe in Kenya they were all hypocrites,' she said, thoughtfully. 'It's all well and good to celebrate together and have meals at one another's houses but there was a clear demarcation when it came to intermarriage. The problem was that some people were old enough to have lived through the partition in India, and the atrocities that occurred there and then still haunted them.'

Smita had studied this terrible era of Indian history at school. In 1947, when the British finally left after three hundred years in India, the country was partitioned into two independent nation states: Hindu-majority India and Muslim-majority Pakistan. Immediately, there began one of the greatest migrations in human history, as millions of Muslims trekked to West and East Pakistan, while millions of Hindus and Sikhs headed in the opposite direction. As a result, communities that had coexisted for almost a millennium attacked each other in a terrifying outbreak of violence, with Hindus and Sikhs on one side and Muslims on the other. The carnage included massacres, mass abductions and savage sexual violence, with seventy-five thousand women raped, and many of them then disfigured or dismembered. By the following year, as the great migration drew to a close, more than fifteen million people had been uprooted, and between one and two million were dead.

'Nonetheless,' Sunita concluded, 'I'm happy to now be living in South Africa, and I'm glad to meet you and your sisters, and a few of Kirit's cousins, so I have new friends here. And I can't complain about my in-laws, as they treat me very well.'

Rumour had it that Sunita had brought with her to the marriage a substantial dowry, left to her in a trust by her father, but who knew if that was true. What she did definitely bring was a talent for the art of henna, or mehndi, application. For Diwali that year, she volunteered to decorate all the girls' hands with the most intricate patterns, and he told Smita that she would be only too honoured to apply the mehndi to her hands and feet on the eve of her marriage to Virat.

Another set of skills that Sunita brought with her were threading and waxing, which were novel methods of hair removal. These she shared privately with Smita, who despaired of the mess and smell associated with shaving and depilating creams. Threading involved manipulating threads of cotton around individual hairs and tugging them off, very much like tweezing, while the sugar-based wax, despite being painful in the execution, left smooth, silky-looking arms and legs on which the hair only grew back after at least a week. Sunita often teased that the pain would be all worth it on her wedding night, when her groom would be amazed at the satin texture of her legs.

Sunita said she'd learnt these skills on a visit to India, where she'd also picked up wonderful beauty tips, like facemasks made from chickpea flour and sandalwood paste that added a magnificent glow to the complexion. That, Smita decided, she would reserve for her wedding day.

As the two young women grew closer, Sunita confided in her new friend. Once, when Smita probed Sunita about her feelings for her husband, she said, 'He isn't the love of my life. I left him behind in Kenya. But at least I did have the experience of falling in love.' Smita, intrigued, asked for details, but Sunita just smiled sadly and said, 'The past should remain in the past. If my in-laws had any inkling of what happened in Kenya, they might send me back, and then I'd be resigned to being an old maid. At least here, I have a chance of having my own children.'

When Smita looked at Sunita inquiringly, her eyes were full of tears.

Over the next few days of mehndi and embroidery lessons – approved of and encouraged by Ma, who was only too happy that her eldest daughter was learning valuable domestic skills – Sunita gradually told her friend the whole story. One of the closest friends Sunita had in Kenya, Yusuf, was a handsome young man whose father owned a clothing store close to her parents' shop. She and Yusuf often walked home together and, as they got older, they developed a secret intimacy and deep feelings for each other.

When Sunita's mother and father were murdered, and she was

sent away to live with her relatives in another town, she furtively wrote many letters to Yusuf but never received a reply. Listening to this, Smita's heart went out to the bubbly young woman: how well she knew the importance of letters from a certain someone! The focus of her life had become waiting every week for the postman's arrival – and, fortunately, Virat's correspondence was frequent and always a joy to receive.

Sunita admitted that she was not truly in love with Kirit, and that she performed the physical act of marriage only to please him; she hoped that she would fall pregnant soon so she would be absolved of performing the act. However, she whispered that when she was with Yusuf, it had been the greatest pleasure her body had ever experienced. Smita was quite shocked at this revelation, so she did not ask any questions and just let Sunita speak. It seemed as if she had all these emotions bottled up and needed to unburden the weight of her past.

Sunita confessed to Smita that she had been so convinced that she would marry Yusuf – that she had already felt married to him, despite not having had the ceremony – that she had yielded to the pleasures that her body demanded. It was just a miracle that she had not fallen pregnant, or she would have ended her life.

This disclosure left Smita dumbstruck and she could not contain her facial expression. Sunita noticed this and apologised for dumping all of this on her new friend. 'There is no one else I could ever share this with,' she said, leaning forward and taking one of Smita's hands in her own small ones.

Regaining her composure, Smita nodded. 'I will never break your confidence,' she promised.

ℬ 13 ℛ

1966: Meeting the in-laws

Even though Smita had confirmed that she and Virat were completely happy with one another, the marriage proposal still had to be finalised. For this, the family planned a trip to his parents' home.

It would be a rushed trip, as Pitaji had commitments he refused to cancel. The October holidays were a busy time for him, and he was asked to performed many prayers. Subha was furious with her husband for prioritising his work above the prospective marriage of their eldest daughter, but her happiness over Smita having found a husband allowed some measure of forgiveness.

Smita was aware of what to expect at Virat's parents' home. He'd told her that they lived modestly compared to her own family, as his father did not have a supplementary income, as Shankar did. He'd written quite boldly in his letters that unless she was willing to forgo some of the luxuries she was used to, she should not marry him.

Smita had been surprised by this blatant offer of an 'escape route' out of the impending marriage, and she'd told Virat that she'd been led to believe that whatever circumstances she was presented with, she would have to accept them. He'd responded that that was an old-fashioned way of thinking, and that he was considering her happiness in the long term, as he did not believe only love could conquer all. Sometimes, this practicality of thinking exasperated her, and she suspected that their marriage would have its fair share of problems because of this trait of her husband-to-be.

Smita didn't think this was going to be a big deal in any case: an outside toilet she could deal with, having been exposed to it at the farm, and although she'd miss hot water on tap, this was quite a recent addition to their own lives, and the Natal winters weren't as severe as those on the highveld, so it wasn't such a great sacrifice. She had little need for other luxuries, and she'd learnt much about being pennywise from Shankar. Still, she felt there was no point in trying to assuage Virat's fears on this point, so she thought she'd just wait for them to be married, then he would see that she was more resilient that he seemed to think.

And, anyway, Virat had told her that he was living with his aunt in her more modern house in Verulam during the week, to be closer to where he was now working, and that they would continue living there after they married, and only go back to Virat's family home over the weekends. In addition, he wrote, his aunt had four young daughters who were all very excited about meeting Smita.

Mr and Mrs Sharma had invited Smita's family for lunch at their home, which meant they would have to brave Natal's heat. With this in mind, Shankar and Subha decided that they would make the trip to the Sharmas' home with Smita alone; the other children could spend the day at their Auntie Maya's home in Durban.

Smita had chosen a simple royal-blue sari with a few sequins for the occasion, and as she wound the metres of fabric around herself, she wondered how this garment had been designed in India, where it was apparently ten times hotter than here. But then, in India they did not have too much consideration for a woman's comfort, she supposed. Men there wore a loose dhoti spun from cotton, with adequate ventilation, and their torsos were bare, which was so much more comfortable and practical. She did her hair in an up-style so that it would not stick to her neck with her sweat.

It was a long drive from Durban to Stanger, and as they neared the Sharmas' home, they passed acres and acres of sugarcane plantations. Glancing at the undulating sea of green, Smita thought of the thousands of Indian labourers who'd been brought here to work in these fields. Her great-grandfather, Subha's father, had arrived on one of the ships to work as a labourer, and after his five-year indenture period, he'd managed to eventually buy land and establish a profitable farm. He was one of the fortunate few who managed to free themselves from the shackles of their British masters but there were many unfortunates who never moved beyond the sugar plantations and whose descendants remained tethered by the chain of poverty.

The family arrived in Stanger on a typical humid coastal summer day which made the clothes stick to the skin and perspiration drip from every inch of the body. Finally, after taking a few wrong turns and some bickering between her parents about whether they should stop and ask for directions, or use the travel map they had in the glovebox, they turned into a gravel driveway flanked by leafy mango trees laden with the glorious, reddish-yellow sun-ripened fruit. Smita longed to bite into the luscious flesh and savour the sweet juice. With all the excitement of the morning, she hadn't eaten properly, and her tummy was sending her some urgent messages.

They drove up to a quaint little wood-and-iron house where a very tense-looking Virat was sitting on the low wall that enclosed the stoep. As soon as he saw the car, he jumped up and approached them, directing her father to a shady spot to park.

Smita's heart leapt into her throat when she saw him in his crisp white shirt and neatly pressed trousers. With his hair slicked back and his smooth-shaven face, she found him quite irresistible. Of course, she'd thought about him almost every minute of every day since she'd first met him, but his actual physical presence now was unnerving.

He opened the door for Subha first and greeted her with his palms together. 'Namaste, auntie and uncle,' he said, grinning sheepishly at Smita and waiting for her father to open her door.

By this time his family had come out of the house, and there were greetings all round. Smita was introduced to Virat's sister, Lata, a quiet woman that seemed to have a constant pained expression on her face, a brother, Varun, who seemed to be as much of an extrovert as Virat was an introvert, and the shy youngest brother, Jay.

Mrs Sharma ushered everyone into the small house, and they all crowded into the modest lounge, which had a long couch against one wall, a wingback chair opposite this, and a bookcase with a radio perched on top against another wall. The lounge had an archway that led to an equally small dining room, with the kitchen on one side and the short passageway to the three bedrooms on the other. Smita knew from Virat's letters that the family often had two of their orphaned cousins living with them as well, and wondered how they all were accommodated in only three bedrooms.

Lata served refreshing ice-cold lemonade, and Smita sipped it while she assessed her surroundings. Among a crammed collection of brass vases, trays and ornaments that seemed to be a mandatory part of the décor in all Indian homes, was a commemorative tray with pictures of the British queen and her consort, Prince Philip, and the wording 'Visit of the Queen of England to South Africa, 1947'.

Following the direction of her eyes, Varun said, 'I see you have noticed one of the most prized possessions in our house. Mother here is quite the Anglophile.'

Smita cringed inwardly but concentrated on keeping a straight face – she didn't want her expression to give her astonishment away.

'As much as we tell Mother that the English were a source of misery for India, and that they plundered and robbed India of all her riches, she loves the idea of English royalty and other English traditions,' Varun continued, unaware of Smita's discomfort.

It was one of the many peculiarities that she would observe in Virat's family – but then, they did originate from Natal, where there was a pride in emulating the English and the proper use of the language, even calling their parents 'Mother' and 'Father' rather than 'Ma' and 'Pitaji'.

'Stop speaking nonsense,' Mrs Sharma said with a smile. 'Virat, take Smita outside and show her the kitchen garden.' Turning to Subha, she continued, 'I was so impressed with Smita's cooking skills when we visited you, and we grow a lot of our own vegetables and herbs here.'

'I'll take her,' offered Varun mischievously, and earned himself a reprimanding look from his mother.

'You can come into the kitchen with me and help there,' she said, sternly.

Virat led Smita by the hand through an impressive vegetable garden planted with rows of spinach, borlotti beans, pumpkins and herbs, and then into a little orchard of mango, guava and lemon trees. 'Maybe they expect us to run around the trees like the lovers do in the Hindi films,' he teased.

Smita blushed at the word 'lovers' but was aware of how her skin sang wherever Virat touched it. Clearing her throat, she said. 'I'm so happy to see you in person again.'

'So do you not enjoy my letters?'

'Of course, but we do need to see each other too,' she said, then added, uncertainly, 'Or are you not excited to see me?'

Virat gave her a disbelieving look. 'Did you not see how happy I was to see you? And you look absolutely beautiful today, even more beautiful than I remembered, and I have been seeing that image every day in my mind.'

His comments made her blush and she quickly changed the subject.

'I wish I could have worn a dress. This sari is hardly practical for this sweltering weather.'

Virat nodded enthusiastically. 'I have been observing some of the young daughters-in-law of my father's brothers, and they have these silly archaic practices of having these young girls almost completely cover their heads with their sari when they talk to the senior men in the family. It's preposterous. Are we still enforcing purdah here in the 1960s when there are revolutions happening all over the world?'

Smita was aware of his liberal ideas from their letters but to hear him express them in person made her admire him even more.

'Anyway, you don't have to worry about that nonsense in our house, as my parents are quite open-minded about these things,' he assured her. 'Varun already has a fiancée, although it is not official yet, and she visits us and wears western clothing all the time.'

Smita could hardly believe how fortunate she was. She was aware that many men insisted on keeping their women all covered up, and she was glad that wouldn't be her after they were married.

Virat, looking suddenly serious and taking both Smita's hands in his, stared into her eyes and said, 'Now, sweet Smita, are you absolutely sure about us?'

His touch made her feel all wobbly inside, but she managed to get out, 'Of course I'm sure. I've told you this repeatedly in my letters. Why you are asking me again?'

'So you're not disappointed about the house?'

'Definitely not. Finally, I can see where you grew up and spend your time. And there is really nothing wrong with your house.'

'Yes, but compared to your father's house – the carpets, the ornate furniture ...'

Smita laughed. 'That is my mother's influence,' she said. 'And, anyway, wherever you are, we will be. We were meant to be together; we were made for each other; I can feel it.'

Virat laughed, then gently pulled her closer to him, with his one arm around her slender waist and the other tilting her head so that he could kiss her. As his lips touched hers, she felt like she would soar up into the clouds, and her cheeks burnt so passionately that it was as if someone had approached her with a brazier of fire.

The midday meal consisted of green banana curry with a deliciously tangy gravy, accompanied by rice and roti, and complemented by dry crisp fried okra and tasty stir-fried pumpkin leaves, almost all the ingredients for which had come out of the kitchen garden.

As Smita munched her way through this scrumptious meal, she surmised that it was going to be difficult to improve on her mother-in-law's cooking.

On the way back to Subha's sister's home, where they planned to spend the night, her parents asked Smita if she would be fine living without all the luxuries she was used to at home. Smita was a little annoyed at this – why was everyone so concerned? Did she behave like a spoiled brat?

'Don't worry, I will manage,' she said, a bit shortly. 'They are all very nice people, and I don't think my mother-in-law will be as evil as some of the ones in the Hindi films, or, for that matter, the stories we hear from our recently married cousins. Remember Rohini's mother-in-law who used to make her do all the housework and cooking, even though she was pregnant, and then not give her enough food to eat, and then used to take all the husband's salary so that she could not buy one thing for herself or her children? Her children always had to wear old clothes while the mother-in-law could have a new sari every month.'

'Now, now, Smita,' chided her father. 'We must not judge from only one side of the story. Maybe your cousin was exaggerating.'

Smita fumed inwardly. Her father always wanted to give people the benefit of the doubt. Why would Rohini make up these stories? She'd looked so haggard and worn out the last time she'd seen her. Rumour had it that her husband beat her as well, but these were topics that were taboo, and Smita knew better than to mention that now.

෨ 14 ଓ

1967: Love is in the air

The house was abuzz with excitement, as Virat was due to arrive soon. Pitaji had gone to fetch him from the train station.

Smita was finding it difficult to concentrate on anything, and was suddenly beset with worry. Haunted by the humiliation of her previous cancelled engagement, she was plagued by feelings of self-doubt and insecurity. Would Virat still be interested in her? Had he seen someone else more interesting in the interim?

Maybe Ma was right when she moaned about living in this isolated, cold dump. If she was in Durban, she could have seen Virat every weekend, and her constant presence would have been a reminder to him of the commitment he'd made and of how happy they were together. As it was, she had to rely on letters and the occasional phone call that he made to her from a call box – naturally, he couldn't make a trunk call from his work, as it was expensive. And although her family had themselves recently acquired a phone at home, it was to be used only in emergencies, as Pitaji had made excessively clear.

Torturing herself, she wondered if maybe at work Virat had met other, more educated women, and they were all as attractive as Miss Simon, and here she was, a simpleton who did not go to any college and who had very little knowledge of the world. In a recent letter he'd asked her if she would want to further her studies, and she hadn't known how to respond. Of course she would, but after her mother's brainwashing, she thought that marriage would end any dream of that kind.

Smita shook her head, resolving to pull herself together and not slip into any sort of melancholy mood or allow these destructive thoughts to pervade her mind. Looking at herself in the bedroom mirror, she whispered to her reflection, 'Chin up,' and gave herself a sweet smile.

Subha's voice floated down the passage: 'You've spent more than enough time dolling yourself up, Smita. Come to the kitchen now. I need your help!'

In the kitchen, her siblings were all excited at the idea of Virat visiting for the week. Her sisters knew that Smita was absolutely smitten, as she pored over his letters at night. Meera thought he was very handsome and had developed an innocent preadolescent crush on him, while for the two little boys, he was the elder brother that they did not have. Meera and Shruthi didn't even mind that they'd have to accommodate their little brothers in their beds in the room that they shared, so that Virat could have a room to himself.

'We're here!' came Pitaji's voice from the front door.

As soon as Smita and Virat saw each other, Smita realised that all her worrying had been for nothing – Virat's eyes filled with love for her, and, as usual, she felt lightheaded and ridiculously happy in his presence.

Over lunch, Virat entertained everyone with stories about the train trip.

'I was a little nervous and distracted at the station, so I went into the first-class carriage by mistake. The conductor was not too friendly when he asked me if I was in the right place, and I was hoping that I would not get into trouble. Luckily, I just mumbled something, and he said my ticket was for second class, where all the other Indians were. I was quite annoyed and remembered Mahatma Gandhi's famous story of when he got thrown off the train as he was in the first-class compartment where only whites were allowed. That was the incident that spurred the Mahatma to fight for equal rights for the Indians in this country.'

'Interesting experiences, Virat,' said Shankar. 'I have not shared my story with my family before, but I also made that mistake once long ago, getting into the first-class carriage, which was reserved for whites, but fortunately the conductor seemed to think that I was white and did not question me. From then on, I tried my luck and always sat in first class, and no one has ever bothered me. It helps to talk to them in Afrikaans, and then they are even more convinced that I am not a coolie, as they like to say.'

Virat, perhaps realising that these stories were probably not suitable for the children, changed his demeanour and described the other highlights of his trip. 'The seat in the compartment was actually turned into a bed that night and all the meals were served on board. It was interesting to watch the landscape change from the window over the twelve-hour journey, from the city to the very green fields and then the drier farmlands, until darkness prevailed. In the morning, you could see the cloud of smog over the towns and cities from all the fires that people lit to keep warm or cook breakfast.' He made it sound so appealing that they all wanted to take the train on their next trip to Durban.

After lunch, Virat played outside with the little boys, kicking a ball around, and making paper boats to float on the huge puddles that resulted from a heavy autumn shower – things that Pitaji never seemed to have the time to do, as he was always working.

During his visit, Smita and Virat talked extensively, albeit always in sight of someone in the family. He told her about his minor brushes with the law after engaging in what some of the students thought were peaceful protests at University College for Indians, where he'd done his undergraduate degree. Initially he used to just observe the protestors, he told her, curious about the causes that they were protesting about. After the Rivonia trial, when Nelson Mandela and his nine co-accused had been sentenced to lifetime imprisonment for crimes against the apartheid government, he had joined the hundreds of other students in a peaceful protest at the university. The police had warned the crowd to disperse, and when this did not happen, they started to threaten to arrest then. Virat was one of the unfortunate ones, and he spent a few hours in a holding cell at the Durban police station.

When his parents got wind of what had happened, they were horrified. Besides being concerned about his safety, there was the worry of his being excluded from university. To send him to university had been a financial strain on the family, which would be alleviated only when Virat had qualified and was earning a salary. It would be a travesty if this did not happen.

Virat was incensed about the political situation in the country and the injustice that was being meted out to the masses, and Smita admired him for his passion – and realised that she felt the same way about many things. But, she told Virat, 'There is no opportunity or medium for me to protest, and, anyway, my parents would be dead against my involvement in anything even remotely dangerous.'

Virat smiled at her. 'I am glad that you do not think that I am overzealous about these things. It is wonderful that we share the same thinking. It is difficult for women to get involved, although there have been some very brave women during the struggle. Some time I will tell you the stories of the valiant efforts of some of these heroes – Lillian Ngoyi, Helen Joseph, Albertina Sisulu, Sophia Williams, Rahima Moosa … There are also some activists in Durban who are women. But, yes, I do understand Smita, and as selfish as it is of me, I shudder to imagine you in jail.' And he held her close and kissed her on the cheek.

Despite the lack of privacy, with at least one pair of eyes on the young couple at almost all times, they managed to get some stolen moments together, whispering sweet nothings to each other, holding hands and stealing furtive kisses. When their passion grew more intense, Smita was horrified to find some angry-looking bruises on her neck. They were both so inexperienced that they did not realise that their desire and lust for each other would result in these telltale marks. How would she explain this to her parents?

Virat was slightly more knowledgeable about these matters and assured her that they would fade after a few days. He was, however, apologetic, and embarrassed as well. If her parents found out, he would be mortified. He told her that he heard that applying toothpaste could help the marks disappear, but this was to no avail.

The only solution was for Smita to feign a sore throat and hide the offending marks under a scarf.

One of the highlights of Virat's visit was when the whole family visited the Joburg Zoo and Zoo Lake, where they hired rowboats.

Smita and Virat claimed a boat for themselves alone, while Pitaji – taking a rare weekend break from his priestly duties – helmed a second one containing his wife and two youngest children, and Shruthi and Meera shrieked and rowed in circles in a third. Eventually they were assisted by the men hiring out the boats when it was apparent that they could not manage on their own.

Although it was a small manmade lake, the expanse of water lent a romanticism to the outing, and Smita couldn't help feeling like she was in one of her Victorian novels. With the sun glistening on the water, her sunhat shading her face and her floral dress draped prettily over her knees, and with handsome Virat rowing the boat with his shirtsleeves rolled up his arms, showing off his muscular biceps, it was just the perfect picture.

Another highlight was when Virat took Smita to visit the University of the Witwatersrand which, when the government had called for universities to be segregated, had taken a stance and actively oppose this injustice. This was, Virat told Smita, unlike the

University of Natal, which now had segregated campuses for whites and non-whites.

They caught the bus there together, and, standing at the base of the columns of the Great Hall, Smita felt inspired. 'Oh, I would so have loved to be able to study here!' she said.

Virat gave her a sharp look, and Smita was suddenly struck with fear. 'Don't worry, my dearest husband-to-be – I want nothing more than to be married to you.'

Virat shook his head, indicating that she'd misunderstood his reaction. 'I'm impressed with your aspirations to study further. I'd be really proud of you if you followed your dreams. You'll have my full support.'

ಸಿ 15 ∾

1967: Wedding shopping

The central focus of the visit to Durban this winter was shopping for Smita's bridal trousseau, Ma told the family one evening over dinner. Durban had many shops that sold Indian wedding attire.

In the Transvaal, Ma was only aware of some travelling salesmen who sold Indian garments. These men visited the Indian areas with their suitcases packed with saris, fancy embroidered skirts and tops, costume jewellery and other trinkets, which they generally bought from the Durban stores. For Ma, this meant paying a higher price for a limited selection and sometimes some very outdated patterns.

Ma's announcement caused a bit of grumbling among the younger siblings, as this would be the second time that a trip to Durban was all about Smita. They would not get to visit their cousins or go to the beach, which were normally the highlights of these visits to Natal. But the younger ones knew that complaining would all to no avail, as Ma was set on getting only the best for the first family wedding.

Smita had come to accept that she might be the lead actress in the drama that was unfolding, but her mother was the director and producer who would dictate the terms and conditions under which she performed. This was Subha's moment in the limelight. She and

Shankar had made a life for themselves in this godforsaken, bleak, ugly, freezing place, and a fairly prosperous one at that, and she could now show everyone what a success her husband was.

The wedding was to be held in the new, recently completed community hall, just up the road from their house, with its shiny mosaic terrazzo tiles that gleamed in the sunlight. Shankar and Subha had sent out invitations to about three hundred families, which included almost everyone in the neighbourhood except the Muslim people – as they ate beef, they would not be welcome at a function where there Hindu prayers were performed. They expected at least four hundred people to attend – many, Subha knew, wouldn't have the means to make the journey from Natal, while others may not come for other, unavoidable reasons, for example, if they were in mourning for a family member who had died.

Subha was aware that there had been some spectacular wedding ceremonies in Durban, with grand décor, and some even had the bridegroom arriving on horseback to mimic the ancient practice in India where the prince arrived on a highly decorated horse or elephant. Of course, they would not go to this extent for Smita's wedding, but it would be a grand ceremony, nevertheless. After all, this had to be an advertisement for her other daughters as well.

The pre-wedding rituals would be held at their house, and Subha insisted that Shankar splash out for it to be repainted inside and out. In order to make space for the marquee in the small back yard, to Smita's distress, the beloved peach tree was cut down. Watching the men with axes chop into its old, gnarled trunk, Smita felt like crying for all the hours of quietude and comfort the tree had provided, not to mention its succulent pink-orange fruit. Subha, however, had no time for sentimentality.

One of the highlights, Subha knew, would be the bridal car. She had forced Shankar to trade in his beloved old Dodge for a brand-new gold Chevrolet before the wedding and this car would turn her relatives green with envy. The day the car arrived, everyone who lived on their street popped out to get a glimpse of this huge, impressive piece of machinery. They watched while Shankar performed the car prayers, to give thanks for the vehicle as well as to ask for protection while driving it.

සො ෆෂ

Even though there would be no visit to the beach or the cinema on this trip, it was always a treat to visit Cato Ridge, and for the children to run in the green fields, indulging the rare opportunity to go barefoot and have the glorious sensation of squelching their feet into the soft warm mud after the crops were irrigated.

Smita realised that this would be her last visit here with her parents, and as she joined her younger cousins on their usual expedition to the nearby stream, she became a little despondent. She watched Ramu playing with the mud, smoothing out a small section with his good hand, then patting it flat with his fisted one. 'See, I'm making patha, like Ma,' he grinned. Her sisters and brothers were having such a wonderful time splashing in the shallow muddy pools searching for tadpoles and just enjoying themselves – these childish games were soon no longer going to be appropriate for her, as she would be a proper grown-up married woman.

In Durban they stayed at Auntie Maya's home, where Smita was glad to see her cousin Rupa, but again she realised sadly that this would be the last time that she stayed with her cousins.

But the next few days were so busy and exhausting that there was very little time to dwell on the past. The sari shops were all concentrated in Durban's 'Indian area', and Smita and Subha soon came to know the salesmen in the various shops, as they cottoned on to the fact that the women were wedding shopping, which would involve the purchase of many saris – not only the wedding sari, but also the sari for the preliminary rituals, saris for the bride's mother and sisters, and the saris that would be in the bride's suitcase that she took to her in-laws' house on the day of the wedding. This would also include saris as gifts for the new mother-in-law, sisters-in-law and any other women living in the house.

Smita had always loved visiting these sari shops, with their dizzying bursts of colour and rolls and rolls of fabric. The shop-keepers were mostly Gujarati and were impressed that Subha could converse with them in their mother tongue. They often laid out savoury snacks for the women, to seem more hospitable and convince them to shop in their establishments.

For the bridal sari, Smita did not want the traditional red – she felt it too common – and they had a difficult time finding something she liked. She also wanted to wear a western-style veil rather than draping her sari over her head, as was tradition. Subha wasn't convinced about this, though, so Smita didn't push it – for now.

Eventually she saw a sari that she instantly loved, in a romantic-looking peachy-pink silk intricately embroidered with ornate little flowers in golden thread. Subha was not thrilled with the choice and tried to convince Smita to choose red or maroon to accentuate her fair complexion, but Smita was adamant. It was really the only decision on which she could exercise her opinion, so she refused to budge. She didn't want to upset Subha, though, so she agreed to wear a red sari for one of the preliminary ceremonies. Subha settled on a stunning blue and gold Benares silk one, so named for the Indian city of Benares, world famous for their elaborate saris.

They selected a beautiful indigo sari for Shruthi, who was now old enough at sixteen to wear a sari, and bought eight-year-old Meera a charming pink skirt and blouse imported from India that had elaborate gold embroidery with sequins. There would be lots of attention on them as well, especially Shruthi, as the matchmakers would be very busy at the wedding. The final sari selections were gifts for Virat's mother, sister and two of his closest aunts.

The blouse fittings for Smita came last, with a choice of pattern on the sleeves and necklines.

When the sari-shopping was finally complete, Shankar took Smita and Subha to their favourite sweetmeat shop in Durban. Here, they bought delicious Indian delicacies that were too complicated or time-consuming to make at home – hot, fresh jalebis with syrup oozing from the glossy orange spirals, creamy white burfi decorated with beautifully coloured slivers of almonds, and the pastel pink and white squares of coconut ice that were always a treat.

Smita was still amused when she saw the sign 'tea room' fronting these shops. They had just inherited the historic names and people still referred to them as such, rather than as cafés, like they called them at home. Of course, later she realised that 'café' was also an anomaly, as it meant coffee in French, but she still thought it sounded much more sensible than 'tea room'.

Shankar needed to get back to work, so Subha agreed that those items that still needed to be purchased – shoes for the bride, for example, and some other odds and ends – could be acquired back in the Transvaal. Pitaji was also muttering about overloading the car and not knowing where all of their purchases would be crammed, even though he had installed new roof racks to allow for all the extra baggage the family would be taking home.

A few days later, it was quite a treat for Smita and Subha to go into Johannesburg with Shankar, where they visited the beautiful double-storey Stuttaford's and John Orr's department stores. 'This is just for the tourist experience,' Subha reminded Smita – she knew things would be cheaper in the Indian shops in Fietas and Fordsburg, where they would go next.

But when Smita spotted the most elegant sandals she had ever seen, with high heels, painted gold and encrusted with gold glitter, she begged her mother to be allowed to try them on – and, to her astonishment, Subha agreed. She felt like Cinderella as the sandals slipped onto her foot. 'Please, Ma!' Smita appealed to her mother. 'Look, they're fifty percent off.'

And when Subha nodded with barely a show of resistance, Smita knew that the gods were smiling down on her.

Next, Pitaji drove his wife and eldest daughter to Fietas, a part of Vrededorp named after the men's outfitters that traded from Fourteenth Street, the area's business street. Here, most shopkeepers and their families stayed in apartments above their shops, but now the apartheid government was forcing them, and Indians living in nearby Fordsburg, to move.

'They want us to go to Lenasia,' one of the shopkeepers complained to Pitaji. 'It's miles from anywhere. Why would we want to go there? All our mosques and temples are here.'

'They're not giving us proper compensation,' another said, angrily. 'And anyway, an old home where there is family history can't be replaced.'

Pitaji listened sympathetically but he felt helpless – he knew, as did the despondent shopkeepers, that it wasn't a battle they were going to win.

Subha brought the glum discussions to an end by clapping her hands. 'We need to get some drapes for the background where the ceremonies at home will take place and to form a backdrop at the community hall,' she said.

At the next fabric shop they went into, Smita spotted a western-style, sheer bridal veil on a mannequin that she simply had to have. Made of a diaphanous fabric and scattered with silver sequins and tiny, embroidered flowers, it was exquisite. Even Subha had to admit, albeit reluctantly, that Smita looked spectacular when the saleslady helped her try it on. Smita was happy with these small victories.

જી ૭૪

With about a week to go until the wedding, Smita received a visit from one of Arvind's dear cousins, who furtively handed her a letter. After their passionate kiss at the Navaratri festival, Smita had avoided Arvind, and had heard later through the grapevine that he'd done well in his exams and had gone to Ireland to study medicine at a university there.

My dearest Smita, the letter read.

I hope that you are well and happy.

I was completely heartbroken to hear that you are actually getting married. You are still the love of my life and I was hoping that somehow you would still be there when I returned. You are my true love and I always hoped with all my heart that I would be the one you would marry. Yes, it is a crazy thought but it has been my dream that this would happen.

Life here is so dreary. The weather is awful, and I miss so much from home – the food, all my friends, family, and most of all you.

We never really got a chance to say goodbye – everything happened in such a rush. My parents insisted that I accept the offer of a place at the university here, and I suppose it will be better for my career. But I always imagined you as part of my future.

Of course, I realise that it was madness to expect you to wait for all those years, but I just wanted you to know how I feel, hoping that you still feel something for me too, and also really hoping that my letter will make a difference to you.

Please think about me before you make your final decision. We could be so happy together.

All my love,

Arvind

Smita felt sympathetic towards Arvind and his plight but she was sure that he would find a suitable girl to marry, either in Ireland or wherever his parents sourced one from, as his family had relatives in many places. She just hoped it would not be a gora, like the one Arvind's cousin had found in England, causing the poor doting parents to excommunicate the cousin; reportedly, the mother had then suffered a stroke and the father had retreated into a deep depressive state at the 'loss' of their only son.

It was bad enough to have any daughter-in-law take over and look after your son but at least with an Indian daughter-in-law you knew what you were getting – unlike with a white girl. 'These white girls all eat beef and show their bare legs in public. They don't know how to cook Indian dishes; our sons will probably never eat roti again!' were just some of the concerns. Indian wives were trained to be subservient and take care of their in-laws as well.

Eventually, after reading and re-reading Arvind's letter several times, Smita decided she would not and could not reply to it. She told his cousin to tell him that she had found her happiness, and to wish him good luck with his career and his life.

ℬ 16 ℭ

1967: A heartbreaking revelation

The pre-wedding week had been particularly busy and Smita felt exhausted. She had forgotten that the wedding itself was simply the culmination of all the preparation and ceremonies performed beforehand. In Natal, Virat would also be having all these pre-wedding ceremonies with his family.

She had, however, cherished her time with her siblings, as moving almost four hundred miles away would obviously mean that she would not see them often. It pained her to think that Ramu would be growing up and she would not witness all the cute things he got up to. Well, she supposed that she would have her own little one soon. The thought made her blush.

Today Smita was sorting out her cupboards, discarding the clothes that she would not take with her and setting aside items she did not need for her sisters, who were at school at the moment, but who would be delighted to come home to substantially supplemented wardrobes. Well into the job, at the back of a top shelf, behind a pile of winter jerseys, her fingers made contact with something that wasn't wool or fabric, and was flat but lightly bulky. It was an envelope, her name written on it in script she immediately recognised as that of her beloved late grandmother, Dadi.

Dadi's letter!

At first, when Dadi had given the sealed envelope to her, just weeks before her death, and she'd hidden it up here, behind her winter woollies, she'd been almost consumed with curiosity and had desperately wanted to open it. But over time she'd forgotten about it. And now, here the letter was! Dadi had told her sternly that she wasn't to open it until she was 'fully a woman' – a vague instruction that, as a fourteen-year-old, she hadn't comprehended.

Turning over the envelope in her hand, she smelt the camphor her grandmother must have enclosed to present insects from eating the paper. 'Dadi, I am about to be married. I am fully a woman now,' she whispered, knowing that the time was right to open the letter.

In the envelope was a one-page letter in Dadi's handwriting, but it wasn't the bold, flowing script she knew from childhood. Spidery and uncertain, it had clearly been written when Dadi was near the end. There were also a few other pages, seemingly torn out of a ledger of some kind, and also covered in Dadi's writing – but in the surer hand that was more familiar to Smita.

My sweet Smita, the letter read.

> *I hope that you listened to your old Dadi and waited to read this letter. I could not tell you this when you were a young girl, but I had to leave my story with someone. I always felt that you were the person I could trust with it.*
>
> *I have enclosed some pages from my journal that I wrote long ago. It will tell you all you need to know. My story, although not a happy one, is a part of where you came from.*
>
> *What you choose to do with this information is up to you, but I beg you please to think carefully before deciding who to tell about it. Your father is the central character in this sorry tale, and I do not wish you to break his heart.*
>
> *You deserve the best, my dear. May God bless you and keep you safe.*
>
> *Your loving Dadi*

Smita shuffled through the journal pages. There were five of them, dated, and closely covered with Dadi's script. The paper was brittle and fragile – even as she handled them, the pages began fragmenting. Their age was confirmed by the date of the first entry.

23 February 1911
We have been on the ship now for 14 days and there is still a long way to go. The baby and I are fine but Lal has been troubled by the sea sickness since we left India.

It is getting much worse now. Maybe the food is affecting him. He is also getting a fever and is complaining of being cold, even though it is very hot here. I am scared and do not know what to do.

I have to keep my strength up as I am also feeding my Krishna and I think that is why he is still fine.

I am writing in English and not Hindi as I would not want any of the people on the ship to be able to read my personal stories. Most Indians cannot read or write English. I was lucky that there were nuns that had a school close to our house, where I was allowed to go until I was 12. I also read my older brother's English books to improve my vocabulary.

24 February 1911
There is a doctor on board, but I have heard he is not good. He is mostly for the indentured labourers, supposedly to ensure they have regular baths and the food is of good quality, but the reality is very different. I have even heard some horror stories from women who have been molested by him, and I will avoid a visit to him if at all possible.

He scares me, with his pale blue eyes and light red hair

and cheeks an angry red from too much sun or maybe too much whisky – I have heard that he likes to drink at night, and then he goes to the latrines and looks for women who are there on their own. Lal is too sick now to accompany me when I go, so a group of other women and I always go together.

Even though Lal and I are having an unpleasant journey, things are much worse for the indentured. There are hundreds of them below decks, crowded together like animals. They are woken every morning at six o'clock, and the women have to help to prepare the meals in the galley, while the men draw the water ration and pour it into wash tubs on the deck. The caste distinctions don't matter on board – high and low castes work together, eat together and clean together.

Passenger Indians like Lal and me, who have paid for our tickets, and the indentured, who have traded their physical labour for their passage, eat similar food.

We paying passengers are offered dry rations to prepare our own meals on deck if we don't want the fare served to the indentured.

For meat-eaters, there are goats in the hold – we saw them being loaded from the dock in Calcutta, and we sometimes hear their cries at night. They are slaughtered from time to time, and sometimes there is fish, but our staple diet is dhal and rice. There are often weevils and dirt in the rice which result in dysentery and diarrhoea in those who eat it.

Due to my Lal's friendly nature, he mingled with the indentured group and sometimes conducted prayers on board for the severely ill and for the unfortunate souls who died during the journey. This is probably how he got sick.

26 February 1911

Lal is sicker by the day and cannot keep any food down. He is dehydrated and needs fresh water to drink, but fresh water is limited in supply. People say that you can get more water if you offer bribes to the sepoys.

I was very scared today and it seemed as if I was going to lose my Lal, as he had a high fever. The other passengers were constantly telling me to take him to the doctor, but I don't want to after all the stories I've heard. Also, we paying passengers have to pay the doctor ourselves for any treatment we receive (the indentured are supposed to get free medical care as part of their contracts).

Finally I had no choice when Lal couldn't even swallow water. I asked someone to go and fetch the doctor. He arrived after an interminable wait and stared at me hard before examining Lal. He listened to his heart, prodded him all over, checked his eyes, pinched his skin. Then he shook his head and asked me if I knew when last he had passed water. Then he said, your husband is gravely ill, I can't attend to him here, we need to get him to the clinic.

I left Krish with a woman I'd made friends with on board, and two kind men helped to carry my poor husband to the small clinic on board, which is just a cabin that has been supplied with medical gear and an examination table. There, the doctor said to me, if your husband doesn't get medication, nourishment and lots of water, he will succumb to the illness. It's a common affliction on board these ships. He is seriously ill. Then he quoted me an astronomical figure to supply this treatment.

I told him we couldn't afford it, as paying for our passage had used up most of our savings. I could not use up the money that my father-in-law had given Lal before we left for the journey. I didn't tell the doctor that I also had a few pieces of jewellery, which I intended to sell when we arrived in South Africa, in order to get transport to the Transvaal and set up our household there. If I'd given the jewellery to the doctor, we would have landed in the new country penniless, and then we would have been in an even worse position than the indentured labourers.

I begged the doctor to help us even though I couldn't pay him, and he said, come with me to the quarantine room and I will show you how you can pay me. At first I did not understand what he was saying, but then, from the tone and the look in his eyes, I realised. My mouth went dry and the bile rose in my throat. I shook my head.

The doctor just shrugged and said, without treatment, your husband will die before sunrise, then you will arrive in South Africa as a poor Indian woman with a baby but no husband. Do you want to save his life or not?

I recalled how widows were treated in India, always considered bad luck and often made to shave their heads and wear white saris to make them appear unattractive. They were often expelled from their homes and subjected to a life of begging. Young widows, such as I would be if Lal died, were often pimped by their male relatives to richer men. My fate as a widow would be worse than death – and I have my baby to think of.

I followed the doctor to the quarantine room, which was another cabin with four bunks in it for sick passengers or crew. He told me to lie down and spread my legs. His smile was terrible and sinister. He was rough but it was over quickly.

When he was finished, he said, get out of here, coolie. I will send the medicine, food and water to your quarters.

He seemed angry with me, which was beyond my com-prehension. My humiliation was total and deep.

30 April 1911

Lal has recovered and I thank God for that but now what seems to be my worst nightmare has come true. I did not get my monthlies. At first I thought it was the stress of travelling and the sea journey but now I'm sick every morning. I am so scared. I have a monster growing inside me.

31 December 1911

I have a new, strong, healthy, beautiful baby son. He is pale-complexioned and has light-brown eyes. Nobody in either Lal's or my family has colouring like this, and Lal has put it down to a blessing from the gods. I am happy for my dear husband to believe this, as the truth would destroy him.

I cannot help but love our baby, who we have called Shankar, as he is a part of me, he has come from inside me. How could I not love him?

My Shankar will shine, and he will be the best son to his father so that he can never fault him.

God must have forgiven me, otherwise I would not have such a wonderful boy.

Smita's heart was pounding in her chest; her hands were shaking and her mouth was dry. Was this true? It seemed absolutely preposterous. Her father was the offspring of some sadistic ship's doctor, the progeny of some vile, disgusting man? How was that possible? Her father was her hero. Not once had he ever shown any signs of violence or bad temper to any of them.

Her Dadi must have been mistaken, Smita decided. She had just miscalculated her dates.

But in her heart, Smita knew the story was true. Shankar's pale complexion – for so long a source of puzzlement but also pride in their family – was finally explained.

And the implications of this – what did it make all of them? She was also quite pale, and so was Ramu. It was all too confusing. And did it matter? Would it change anything?

She was one-quarter white, she suddenly realised. The thought of it made her skin crawl. Whites were so foreign; they ate meat, and they were so cruel to those who did not look like them. And they certainly did not acknowledge people who were half-castes or not of pure race: the entire coloured community was testament to that.

Why had her grandmother been so insistent on passing on this knowledge, rather than just forgetting it, letting it go, letting it get lost in time? It made no difference now: her father was a respected priest in the community.

Shaking her head gently, Smita knew that it would not benefit anyone to know this story. Her grandmother, for reasons she couldn't know and didn't understand, had passed on this burden to her; but she would take it with her to her grave.

Tearing Dadi's letter and the fragile ledger pages into shreds, she concealed them in her pocket. No one would notice when she added the scraps to the cooking pit created for the huge amounts of food that her mother and aunts would be preparing for the pre-wedding feasts.

৪০ 17 ରେ

1968: Rituals and matrimony

Subha had seemed to acquire superhuman powers in the few weeks before the wedding, throwing her considerable energy and skill into preparing all the treats and pickles and condiments that would accompany the main meals.

She did have continuous support from the neighbours and other close relatives, and the house was in a state of permanent hustle and bustle. The ladies of the community were always there, assisting with peeling and chopping vegetables, and the fastidious and time-consuming job of picking the rice, lentils and beans – removing damaged grains and tiny stones which, should a guest bite into one, would have been mortifying for the host.

There had been considerable activity outside as well. The marquee was delivered and had to be erected in the back yard. Subha insisted on supervising that as well, and loudly congratulated herself on her foresight in having had the peach tree removed. 'The stump will serve nicely as a seat for you when the prayers and rituals are performed,' she told Smita. 'We can decorate it with some pretty fabric and put a cushion on it. It will be perfect.'

৪০ ରେ

The thanksgiving prayer to invoke the blessings of the gods a week before the wedding marked the beginning of the feasting and the entertaining of guests.

Subha had invited Shankar's brother and his family from Germiston and the close neighbours, as well as all the ladies who'd helped Ma with the papad and the preparation for the wedding feast. Subha's Natal family would only arrive a few days before the wedding, as the men could not take too much time off work.

Smita prayed with the utmost sincerity, as she was truly thankful that God had delivered Virat to her so easily. Her story could have been like Sunita's: forced to marry a man for financial reasons, convenience and pressure.

All the sweetmeats, savoury snacks, pickles and other goodies that Subha and the neighbourhood women had been preparing over the previous weeks and months would form part of the sumptuous spread offered to the guests after the prayer, with the hope that they would be suitably impressed by the superior quality of these offerings.

Finally, with just two days to go before the big day, the family from Natal began to arrive. The closest relatives – Subha's mother, and Auntie Maya, and Smita's cousins – stayed at their house, with many others being accommodated in the various neighbours' homes. They had laid mattresses and piles of blankets and duvets on the floor of the bedrooms to accommodate the children and teenagers, while the adults slept in the beds.

With the arrival of Rupa, it was time for the bride-to-be and her favourite cousin to gossip and giggle. The youngest of five sisters, Rupa had watched all of them draping their saris and applying their makeup, and had learnt some valuable skills; she could now accentuate a woman's most attractive features and mask the less appealing ones. She also was talented at creating beautiful hairdos, which was just as well, as Smita would require at least three different styles. For the mehndi, the henna-applying ceremony, it would be simple locks; the night before the wedding would require braids and a bun; and for the wedding itself, it would be a regal beehive with a little tiara holding the veil in place.

Smita knew that she needed to make the most of looking and being treated like a queen, as immediately after the wedding she would have to slip straight into the role of serving her husband and his family, so her status would tumble down pretty rapidly. Subha, either realising this, or simply uncharacteristically relaxed thanks to the relief and elation of having Smita finally betrothed, had excused her eldest daughter from most of the domestic kitchen and household chores in the last few weeks. This reprieve for Smita was a curse for her younger sisters, as they were next in line to be subjected to their mother's training.

After the peaceful and spiritual experience of the prayer, the day of the mehndi was dedicated to merriment and laughter. It was done in the marquee, where a backdrop of colourful saris and glittering tinsel was created, and a small dais for Smita to sit on was erected with old, discarded crates. Many of the older women sang folk songs with improvised bawdy lyrics that turned Smita's face the colour of her crimson sari but that only encouraged them further, resulting in gay laughter from everyone.

All the women were in awe of Sunita's finesse with her mehndi equipment, and the exquisite patterns she created. She started by covering Smita's palms in intricate lines that eventually resembled flowers with intertwining stems interspersed with little dots, paisley patterns and hearts swirling up past her wrists and ending at the elbows. She repeated the intricate, delicate designs on Smita's feet and ankles. The depth of the colour was supposed to indicate the level of passion of the bride, and Smita blushed at some of the comments made while Sunita applied the henna.

A common practice was to hide the groom's name within the intricate patterns, and for the groom to have to find it on the wedding night. Smita indicated the spot on her arm where Sunita should hide the name, ignoring the giggling suggestion that she conceal it on her thigh or above her breasts.

To protect the mehndi patterns and ensure that they did not lose their colour once the excess henna had washed off, Sunita dabbed them with lemon juice and sugar, and slipped plastic bags over Smita's hands and feet. Smita then had to be fed her supper and needed assistance when using the toilet, to the amusement of her younger sisters. 'Your turn will come!' she warned them, feeling a little irritated at how much inconvenience she was being expected to endure.

But she softened when she realised how impressed Shruthi and Meera were with Sunita's stunning work, and how in awe of their elder sister. 'It is so beautiful! I cannot wait for my turn!' said Meera, marvelling at the results when the dried and cracked henna paste was carefully washed off the next morning, revealing a bright deep-burgundy design. Smita herself was amazed at the loveliness: the mahogany colouring of the dried henna paste against Smita's creamy skin was truly breathtaking.

The next day – the eve of the wedding – was a mixture of fun and prayer and some ancient rituals during which the womenfolk prayed to the ancestors and asked for their blessings. The blessing of the earth goddess was invoked, asking her to protect the bride in her new home. The ladies would go to a spot outside the bride's home and use a hoe to dig up some soil, which would be blessed before being used as part of the base on which the sacred fire was lit for the wedding ceremony.

This ritual was an opportunity for the women to sing and dance to the beat of a handheld drum, away from the prying eyes of the menfolk. Smita could not accompany them as this was a ritual only for the married women, but she heard the inharmonious singing from her bedroom and was amused at the way these normally stern old women let themselves go the first chance they got.

When the ladies returned from the ritual, it was time for the purification ceremony for the bride. Virat had undergone a similar ceremony at his parents' home and Smita felt warmth infuse her body at the thought that they had the same experience even though it was not at the same time: Virat had had to have his purification ceremony earlier, as they spent the day before the wedding driving to the Transvaal. He and his parents were spending the night at the home of some distant relatives in Lenasia. It was tradition that the groom and bride were prohibited from meeting the day before the ceremony.

For the ceremony, raw turmeric, an ancient ayurvedic remedy for various ailments, was crushed and mixed into a paste with various oils, and applied to Smita's face, arms and legs, to purify her mind and body, to cleanse her skin and remove dead cells, and to soothe and calm any pre-wedding jitters.

Her older female cousins were quite merciless, inserting their hands into her blouse, and pinching and tickling her on her back, her upper arms, her legs and chest.

'We need to smear it nicely on your neck and chest so that you will be glowing everywhere,' one giggled.

'Yes, we need to make your whole body beautiful for your new husband,' said another.

'Then he won't be able to resist you …'

'… and you won't be so pale all over!'

The women were making Smita quite nervous with all their banter, and their lewd comments were making her a little uncomfortable. She was thankful that turmeric was also used to alleviate anxiety and hoped it would do its work.

Supper was now ready. The food, cooked by Ma and the women in the community, was served by her cousins and youngsters in the neighbourhood who were always willing to help.

After she'd eaten, Smita retired early to her room, feigning fatigue, and she could hear the loud music coming from the marquee, the laughter of guests and, above it all, the sound of the popping rice from the small gas cooker set up in a corner specifically for this purpose. According to tradition, the respective families had to provide a portion of popped rice on the day of the wedding. These were mixed to symbolise the merging of the two families and given to the bridal couple to offer into the sacred fire that they would circumambulate.

Later, Smita ventured out as she could not resist the music and laughter that she knew followed the dancing that her sisters and cousins were engaged in. They were thrilled to see her and made a human circle around her, taking turns twirling her around until she was dizzy.

In bed that night, after everyone had gone to bed, Smita tossed and turned. She knew she needed proper rest to have all her faculties operating optimally, and she didn't want to miss any part of her wedding ceremony or to have her concentration lapse during this, one of the most important days of her life thus far, just because of lack of sleep. However, the inviting call of slumber did not arrive; she was much too preoccupied. Would it all go as perfectly as they had planned? she wondered. Was she making the right decision when it came to her husband-to-be, or was it infatuation and would it wear off with time? Did this thing called love really exist or was it a figment of the imagination, something that authors made up to enthral desperate young women who longed for their dreary lives to change? Would she end up like her mother, who sometimes appeared bitter and disillusioned?

Turning over and plumping up her pillow for the umpteenth time, Smita decided she had to have a stern word with herself. She was not as expectant or demanding as Subha, and was far more of an optimist, and she did not let her circumstances rule her emotions. With these bracing thoughts she must have fallen asleep, as the next thing she knew, the sun filtering through the gap in the curtains and a slight breeze was creating variegations of light to dance on the wall of her bedroom.

Stretching luxuriously, she listened to the noises coming from the kitchen, where her mother would be making a sweet rice pudding for her – the token last meal she would eat that was cooked by her mother. One of her mother's brothers would feed it to her, as was customary, and she would share it with her sisters and unmarried cousins, symbolising the last meal she would eat as a single woman.

Her heart began beating faster and harder than normal, from excitement and nerves. She was just swinging her legs out of bed when Rupa stormed in. 'Stop dreaming, Smeets! We need to transform you into a princess, remember, and the way you look it is going to take a long time!' Rupa laughed at her own joke, then continued, 'Come, let's go and get some sweet rice, then we can start the painting and sculpturing. Sunita said she is coming at half seven, and it is already ten past.'

Smita had to be bedecked in the sola shringar, the sixteen items that beautified her body and face to make her irresistibly desirable to her new husband. The mehndi, already done, was the first of these; she still had to have a bath in perfumed water and be doused with perfume so that she had a most sensual scent; then, traditionally, sandalwood paste would have been applied to her face and body but these days makeup had to suffice.

The highlight was the draping of the gorgeous wedding sari and the addition of the bridal jewellery, which included an intricately carved necklace and hand jewellery, countless bangles, earrings, a nose ring, and anklets that made a sweet jingling sound as she walked. She also had little dots decorating the curves above her eyebrows, and eyeliner and kohl, of course, which in addition to accentuating her almond-shaped eyes would serve to ward off the evil eye that could be cast on her by any person who was jealous of her or wished her harm.

Rupa and Sunita finished the process in record time – Smita stood in front of the mirror, almost struck dumb by the transformation:

she looked exactly like a princess from medieval India as depicted on the silver screen.

Anil, a neighbour's son, arrived in her father's new car to fetch her. The car was decorated with freshly cut marigolds, foil ribbons, balloons and streamers. She was driven the short distance up the road to the community hall.

There, she stepped into the aisle created between the seated guests to make her way to the canopy where the ceremony would take place. Walking slowly and carefully – she was wearing high heels, her sari was heavy, and her vision was partly obscured by the veil – she felt her chest tighten with nerves. But then she glanced up at Virat, waiting under the canopy for her, and he looked back at her with so much adoration in his eyes that she immediately calmed down.

When she was finally standing next to him, he lifted the veil and they garlanded one another, symbolising their mutual acceptance, respect and love. The garlands, little floral masterpieces, had been created by stringing together alternating pairs of fresh carnations and roses punctuated with baby's breath.

Next, her parents did the symbolic giving away of their daughter to her husband – supposedly one of the greatest gifts Hindu parents could give, as they were handing over an incarnation of the goddess Lakshmi to another household. Smita never quite understood the contradiction in this: if the woman was such a precious gift, why did the dowry system, which dictated that the groom's family receive financial compensation as well as extravagant gifts from the bride's parents in return for allowing their son to marry her, exist in ancient and in some instances in current India? When she'd asked her father about this once, he'd told her that there is no sanction of any demand for a dowry or cash in the scriptures; it was an evil that had crept into society and been manipulated by people in the name of religion.

The priest chanted the Vedic mantras that prescribed the rituals that were to be performed and explained each of them in detail to both the bride and the groom, to emphasise the importance of the vows. The Vedic mantras originated in scriptures believed to have been written in 1500 BCE and which informed the practice of Hinduism.

In one of the most momentous rituals of the ceremony, Virat led Smita through the seven sacred steps, clasping her hand tightly. They both listened to the significance of each step, symbolising the seven promises made to each other: to pray for provisions for their household; to develop their physical, mental and spiritual powers to lead a healthy life; to earn a living by righteous and proper means; to acquire knowledge, happiness and harmony by mutual love, respect, understanding and faith; to strive to have children for whom they would be responsible – here, Virat smiled at Smita and she felt herself blushing; for self-control and longevity; and to be true to each other and remain lifelong companions.

Then came the circumambulation of the sacred fire, or hawan, by the bridal couple. The fire was fuelled with ghee and wooden sticks to evoke Agni, the fire god, who served as the divine witness to the ritual. At this point Smita, who had initially been on Virat's right, moved to his left side, indicating that she was now closer to his heart. The puffed rice was then added to the fire, and the new wife prayed for long life for her husband and for a marriage filled with peace and harmony.

Virat applied the sindoor to the parting of Smita's hair and placed a red dot in the centre of her forehead. This was to bestow good fortune on the bride, and activated the chakras that represented spiritual connection to herself and others, although many people joked that this was similar to a stop sign, so that when a man other than her husband approached her, he would immediately see the red 'stop sign' and back away.

The concluding prayers and the peace prayer brought the ceremony to an end, and Virat was whisked off to eat with the men, a preposterous tradition that annoyed Smita for what it represented, and for the inequity of the treatment of the bride and groom. The new son-in-law and his closest relatives were seated at a designated table at the front of the hall and given gifts of cash, gold coins and jewellery – a continuation of the dowry principle, a gesture that the family was so grateful to the groom for relieving them of their burdensome daughter that they treated him with utmost respect.

Smita, meanwhile, had her meal in the little dressing room at the side of the hall where no one could see her, and she was definitely not showered with any gifts. Her mother, sisters and cousins all fussed over her, though, and Subha even fed her, as Smita's hand jewellery made it difficult for her to do this herself.

Smita, almost overcome with emotion, protested that she couldn't eat much. 'Ma, please stop. My tummy has a funny feeling and my mouth is dry.'

'That is just nerves,' her mother scoffed. 'You must eat. You have a long journey ahead. Just have some of the dessert so it can sweeten your mouth and your feelings for your husband.'

Smita, touched by her mother's enthusiasm and concern, suddenly felt a lump in her throat as she reflected on the trials and tribulations of Subha's life, including how she had always lived far away from her beloved family, and her six pregnancies and the death of her twins. Subha was a creature of her time, and adamant about her views of the world, so she could not appreciate the changes and opportunities that women were afforded now. Smita smiled up at her mother. She hoped that one day she would be able to show her how things could be different.

Finally, the guests got their chance to congratulate the couple and shower their blessings on them. After this hour-long ordeal of hand-shaking, kissing and hugging, Smita's cheeks were strained from all the smiling and the thin straps of her beautiful new sandals were etching deep streaks into her soft hennaed feet. But these minor discomforts were forgotten when her family came up to the bridal couple to say goodbye.

Her sisters were trying hard not to cry but when Ramu ran to Smita and clutched her around the legs, the tears flowed quite freely amidst the laughter. Virat gently picked up Ramu and high-fived him. 'I am sure that you all will visit us soon. So sorry for taking away your sister but at least there will be somewhere to have a holiday and we can go to the beach and have lots of fun,' Virat assured them all.

There were a lot more tearful hugs and kisses, then it was time to leave. With a final hug to her parents, Smita got into Virat's father's car, driven by his brother Varun, to leave her childhood home behind. They were followed by a few other cars filled with Virat's relatives, who would accompany them to the airport before embarking on the long drive home to Natal.

℘ ℭ

As the cars moved slowly along the neighbourhood streets, with the various drivers honking their horns loudly to proclaim that there was a matrimonial procession moving through, some of the younger boys followed on foot, throwing confetti and coloured rice at them. Smita glanced through the open window at the familiar houses as they passed through the streets, finally reaching the periphery where the less affluent residents lived. When they reached Kanamma's house, and Smita saw the old lady standing outside, she called for Varun to stop.

Kanamma, smiling serenely, came over. She was holding a small bunch of fragrant fresh flowers, which she scattered over the car as a blessing. 'Go well, my child,' she said quietly through the car window. 'You will get all you have wished for. You are a good girl, helping your mother all the time, and now the gods are smiling down on you.' She gently squeezed Smita's arm, waved at them and backed away.

Then they were on the highway on their way to the airport – the tickets had been a very generous gift from her father, to save the bridal couple from the arduous hours-long journey by car – and the houses were left behind. Smita glanced around at the landscape of depressing mine dumps and felt glad that she would not have to be exposed to this unsightliness any more. She looked so forward to always seeing lush green vegetation and occasionally the sea.

As she thought about this, she felt Virat's body relax next to her – she'd been so self-absorbed that she hadn't noticed that he was also very tense. Now there would always be another person to consider, she thought, giving his hand a comforting pat and smiling at him, and someone to share her problems with. 'I am sorry, Virat, for all the tears,' she said. 'This is the happiest day of my life, but it is also a big change, you know. And it is a little scary too. Also, I am so tired. And you must be too.'

Virat put his finger on her lips. 'Shh, Smita, please don't start apologising for no reason. Yes, you are tired, and you must be uncomfortable, too, in that sari and all the jewellery. It must be scary to leave your family behind – you are still young. But don't worry, I will do everything in my power to make you happy.'

With that, he protectively put his arm around her and drew her close to him. Smita rested her head on her husband's shoulder, and he gently clasped her hand under the folds of her sari.

Epilogue

1984

As the resounding recording of 'Gaudeamus igitur' reverberated through the brightly lit auditorium, Smita, sitting at the front of the gathering with the other three hundred graduates – most of whom were much younger than her – became misty eyed. Even though she did not understand all the Latin lyrics, the timbre of the voices, the acoustics of the venue – the Main Hall of the University of Durban-Westville – and the tone of the song elicited a feeling of pride and achievement, causing a tightness in her chest and raising goosebumps on her skin. She was a little dismayed to see a smidgen of mascara on the tissue she was using to stem her tears and hoped that the damage was not too serious. She did not want to look like a raccoon when she posed for her photographs.

Her focus shifted to the imposing parade of esteemed academics in their voluminous gowns billowing past in a riot of colour, bright scarlet, royal blue and rich purple, trimmed with brocade or satin. As much as she admired them, it seemed like a journey to the medieval era, and to her it did not quite make sense. Tradition was an important part of any ceremony, of course, but still it felt to her like an unnecessary adherence to colonial times – not to mention that the procession was made up of largely white males.

Still, she thought, as she glanced behind her at the rows of other students, about a third of the students were women, and there was as decent smattering of black and brown people. Progress was being made. And here she was herself, proof that things were changing.

When her name was called, she proudly strode onto the stage for her scroll to verify her achievement of her Master's degree in education. Quickly stealing a glimpse out at the audience, to the area where her family was seated, she saw her mother beaming and enthusiastically applauding her as she was capped with the conventional mortarboard by the chancellor and then conferred the appropriate sash by a second university official.

Her family – who was definitely now making the most noise, with their clapping and cheering – included not only her parents, and her sisters and brothers, but also Virat and their twelve-year-old daughter, Kirthi.

Her son, Kumar, was too little to sit through a ceremony like this, so, to his chagrin, had had to stay at home with the babysitter, but he'd been placated with a rented VHS cartoon movie and an excessive number of sugary products.

While Subha had not said much in the way of congratulating Smita on the eventual earning of this hard-won degree, her insistence on driving all the way from Bakerton, in spite of the discomfort caused by her arthritis, to attend this ceremony spoke volumes. And she'd brought with her a gift of a stunning cream and gold sari that she'd asked – not insisted – Smita to wear at the ceremony.

And there had been other spin-offs back home in Bakerton to Smita's insistence on studying further, and Virat's obvious approval and support of his clever wife. Shruthi had been allowed to pursue a degree in psychology, while Meera had followed in her father's footsteps and was a successful teacher. It seemed that Subha had finally realised and acknowledged that if husbands wanted educated wives, then they had to ensure that their daughters were not left behind in the modern world.

Smiling down at her mother in the sea of people, Smita thought that maybe now, after all these years, she would acknowledge that a woman could have it all.

Glossary

Aarti: Hindu ceremony involving the offering of light to deities.
Baleta: Piggyback.
Beti: Daughter.
Bhai: Brother.
Bhajan: Song of praise.
Bhagwan: God.
Bhuthin: Female ghost.
Charpoy: Lightweight cot made of a frame strung with light rope.
Daggarokers: person that habitually smokes marijuana (dagga)
Dhoti: White scarf tied into loose pants.
Diwali: Festival of lights; a celebration that marks the triumph of good over evil.
Dokhla: Steamed spicy wheat cake.
Gora: White person.
Hawan: Ritual fire.
Hurdee: Turmeric.
Jalebi: Fried confection drenched in syrup.
Kheer: Rice pudding.
Khuri-kitchri: Spiced yoghurt dish.
Kirtan: Narration of religious story, typically in song form.
Manja: Turmeric.
Mehndi: Henna.
Moksha: Salvation.
Nalangu: Ceremony performed before a wedding to purify the couple.
Panchang: Hindu calendar.

Papad: Deep-fried cracker.

Patha: Deep-fried side dish made from amadumbi leaves.

Pitaji: Father.

Pitrpaksh: Period characterised by rituals performed to pay respects to the dead.

Puja: Religious ritual.

Puri: Deep-fried unleavened bread.

Rakhee: Red thread tied around the wrist of a boy typically by his sister.

Sepoy: Indian soldier.

Seviyan: Dessert made using thin rice/wheat noodles boiled in spiced and sweetened milk, served with nuts and dried fruit.

Seedha: Remuneration given to Hindu priest, generally in the form of grains, cloth, money.

Sindoor: Traditional vermilion powder worn by married women along the parting of their hair.

Thali: Flat silver plate.

Yajna: Hindu ritual performed in front of a sacred fire.

Acknowledgements

Producing a book is an arduous but exciting journey, and this one would not have been possible without the help of many people.

First and foremost, thank you to my publisher, Colleen Higgs, and the team at Modjaji for having faith in my manuscript.

A huge thank you to my editor, Tracey Hawthorne, for her insight and careful editing, as well as the team that assisted in producing the final polished version of the novel.

Thanks to Maren Bodenstein for the initial edits and steer on the story development.

I am so grateful to Carla Kreuser for producing the gorgeous and insightful artwork on the cover.

I thank my parents, Kishore Juggath for his initial editing of the manuscript and my mother, Shakuntala Juggath for sharing some of her interesting childhood memories with me.

I really appreciate the time that siblings and some of my very close friends spent on reading early versions of the book and egging me on through the process.

Finally, I am very grateful to my incredible husband, Bava Pillay, for his ongoing support and encouragement, and for always being there for me.

About the author

Ashti Juggath grew up on the beautiful KwaZulu-Natal North Coast. Often during school holidays, she spent time with her grandparents in Springs on the East Rand, the predominant setting for her first novel. She has a Master's degree in Pharmacy and works as a pharmacist for a large corporate in the City of Gold. *Peaches and Smeets* is her first novel, which she wrote believing that the stories of the past needed to be captured for posterity. Ashti currently lives in a leafy suburb in Johannesburg with her husband, three children and many books.